Money Kings

Just Like Daddy 2

THOMAS LONG

Cover designed by Trendsetter Publications
www.tspubcreative.com

DEDICATION

This book is dedicated to the memory of my young cousin, Larry James Hooker, Jr. During the course of me completing this book, he lost his life senselessly as another casualty of the violence that plagues young black men in the streets of Baltimore. Only 23 years old, you were just a baby in this world when you were taken away. You were just another man-child in the Promised Land, ill-equipped to survive in a savage world that feasts upon our young. I pray that your death awakens the conscious of another young soldier fighting in the wrong war of self-destructive behavior. I pray that he chooses to become a soldier in the war for the salvation and uplifting of a generation sincerely in need of proper guidance. May your soul find peace in the hereafter.

Other titles available by Thomas Long:

Dayvon's Story: A Thug's Life
Just Like Daddy
Takeisha's Song: Cash Rules Everything
The Guilty Pleasures Series (erotic short series)
Good Wood (erotic short story)

Coming soon:

Unconventional Love
The Bodymore Homicide Novella Series, Volume 1: Jericho Jones: The Smooth Assassin

The Bodymore Homicide Novella series, Volume 2: Blood Diamondz

The Bodymore Homicide Novella series, Volume 3: Psycho Chick

Steamy City Nights (erotic short stories)

You can also find out additional information on Thomas Long at:

www.tlongwrites.com

http://www.tlongwrites.com/apps/blog

Facebook: www.facebook.com/tlongmoney

Twitter and Instagram: @tlongmoney

Prologue

It had been almost six months since Polo died. The streets of Baltimore were wide open for a new king to be crowned. Polo had a long reign as the major shot caller for over twenty years in one of the most drug-infested cities in America. He was genuinely perceived in the underworld and in the legitimate business community as a stand-up dude. He got a lot of love and respect out in the streets from the young up and coming hustlers as well as the OG cats. The police department loved him because he managed to keep the murder rates down in the areas where he operated his drug business. His deep pockets and willingness to contribute generously to the political campaigns of many local politicians insulated him well from facing criminal prosecution for his illegal activities. He was smart, and an astute businessman with excellent negotiating skills.

Polo had managed to flood the streets with the highest grade cocaine and heroin, at the cheapest prices, thanks to his South American and Middle Eastern drug connections. All the mid-level dealers in the city copped their work from him because nobody could beat his prices. He had a monopoly on the wholesale distribution drug game, with the exception of a few small distributors on the outskirts of the city. Now that he was dead and his whole crew dismantled, everybody was thirsty for that prime time work. It was drier than a desert out on the streets. Drug crews scrambled to no end to find coke or dope that was at least half the purity and good quality as what Polo had supplied.

The crack heads and junkies were in a panic because the product that they were getting was diluted garbage. It was cut and stepped on so many times that they couldn't even get high off of what they bought. All the city's hustlers were desperate to get their hands on some of that good work. It was a recession like the streets hadn't seen in years. That was where JR knew he could step in and fill that void.

While business was tanking for everyone, JR's crew hadn't missed a beat since Polo was gone. His corners stayed jumping all day and night with the fiends coming back and forth to cop more of that good boy and girl. The Colombian connection that he established in New York while conducting business on Polo's behalf kept his pipeline to the best cocaine intact. JR was situated perfectly to step right into the role as the new Boss on the throne. He had access to the top notch coca that everybody wanted to get their hands on, and he could get it for dirt cheap from his Colombian connection, Julio Gomez.

JR had also established a working relationship with a drug supplier from Afghanistan, who had agreed to supply him with premium Middle Eastern heroin. He knew him simply as Ahmed. JR had already negotiated how much he would pay per kilo of raw coke and dope, as well as the amount that he would have to kick back to Julio and Ahmed for their consignment arrangement, if he were to increase his shipments to include not just product for his crew, but the entire city of Baltimore. He was asking for a ton of weight from both of them, but he was confident that he could move the product at a rate that would make their relationship mutually beneficial for all parties.

All that was left for him to do at this point was to get all of the top hustlers in the city on board with his plan, and he would be set for life. He knew that would be the easy part of the job. To convince a true hustler to buy some good quality narcotics at a dirt cheap price was about as easy as convincing a hooker to sell pussy to a john willing to pay twice her asking price. They had no choice but to go along with his plan or starve. He held all of the cards. JR could see himself being larger than street legends like Little Melvin, Peanut King, and Rudy Williams combined, if everything went smoothly. He had called a meeting today with all of the city's top bosses to lay out his plan for total domination of the Baltimore city drug trade.

"Boss, are you sure that this plan is gonna work?" Demon asked as he steered the Cadillac Escalade through the busy Bmore streets, en route to the meeting spot.

Demon Walker's name fit him just right; he was evil as Satan since the day he was born. His youth was filled with violent episodes that constantly landed him in juvenile detention centers. Committing murder gave him an erection. Just the thought of maiming a fool got him excited. He was born to kill and destroy. Standing an imposing six feet four inches tall and weighing nearly three hundred pounds, he was a highly skilled killing machine. He was a fifth degree black belt in karate and a deadly sharpshooter. Before he came to work for JR, he was a bouncer at several strip clubs in Baltimore. Working as a bouncer at strip clubs was a genuine waste of time and his talent. After JR saw him lay out four dudes at a club one night, he approached him about joining his team. With limited options, JR's offer was one he couldn't refuse. He became JR's head of security and first man to call whenever someone got out of line and needed a dose of act right in their life.

"Hell yeah, it's gonna work. If these fools wanna stay in business, it would be smart of them to fall in line with The Boss. Ain't no way they're gonna find a better deal than what I'm putting on the table," JR replied confidently. He had contemplated his plan thoroughly, thinking it through from all angles.

"What about them fools that's gonna be suspicious, thinking that you had something to do with Polo's death? The streets are talking, and everybody ain't buying the story that Polo was killed by them NY boys. A lotta cats had a lotta love for Polo. I mean, how is it gonna look with him gone and now you're trying to step into his shoes?" Diggy asked from the front passenger seat.

Diggy was JR's top underboss. He handled all of the day-to-day interaction with the street level workers in the organization. He made sure they had work and that their count came back right at the end of each shift. He was a loyal soldier and followed JR's directions to the letter. He studied his every move like a wise apprentice who studied at the foot of a master. When it was his time to take the seat at the top, he would be well prepared.

"I don't give a fuck what they believe. Polo is dead, in the dirt, and a non-motherfucking factor. I'm here, live and in the flesh, with that work. If they wanna get paid, they're all gonna fall in line and recognize that I'm that nigga with the keys to the vault. If somebody feeling bold and wanna bring us a move, we're gonna handle that ass accordingly," JR pronounced boldly. He spoke with conviction and the passion of a born leader.

JR insulated himself with a cadre of hungry young lions ready to kill for that scrilla. Demon trained them well to be judge, jury, and executioner when holding court out in the streets. If anyone was foolish enough to test his hand, the murder game would be administered without mercy by his wolves. Simply put, JR did not play when it came to dishing out hurt to make his point. Mothers, fathers, children, and even the dog could get it if you stood in the way of his money.

"Boss, you know I'm down for whatever. I ride or die with you until the end," G Money said eagerly.

G Money always went out of his way to kiss JR's ass, as though it would gain him special favor with The Boss. The rest of the crew clowned on him behind his back because of his brown nosing. Despite his faults, he had proven himself to be a money getter and stand up soldier, which was why JR kept him around. Having those two qualities made him a valuable asset to the organization.

"Man, I ain't stuntin' none of these fools. Let's get this paper! D, make a right at the next corner and pull up into the parking lot of the car wash," JR yelled over the loud music.

They had reached their destination. JR had called the meeting at his all night car wash, Exquisite Custom Detailing Services. Since it opened, business had been steady with a large profit margin. Melissa Epson, G Money's mother, was the official owner as far as the city was concerned. This was the perfect place to hold a meeting. The in and out traffic was always heavy with both young drug dealers and regular citizens getting their whips shined up. Their meeting could be conducted inconspicuously without attracting the kind of unnecessary attention it would garner had it been conducted somewhere else.

As JR glanced across the parking lot, it looked like a car show with all of the Benzes, BMWs, and other high-end European whips that were filtered throughout the lot. He recognized a few of the whips as belonging to just the men he wanted to see. All of the other bosses had arrived on time for the meeting. JR made it a point to be 30 minutes late, as a power move to signify that they were all on his time and he would be calling the shots. He knew a few cats would be tight about having to wait, but he didn't give a fuck. This was his show.

When Demon parked the truck in JR's reserved spot, all of the other bosses got out of their automobiles and proceeded to the main office area of the car wash. Daps and pounds were exchanged amongst them as a sign of respect. Some of the cats had beef with each other from the streets, but that was put on pause at JR's request, at least until this meeting was over.

In total, there were five major players invited to attend this crucial meeting of the minds. They were Big Slim from Westport, Money Marvin from Northeast Baltimore, Prince from South Baltimore, Bop from the Caroline Street area, and Fat Chris from Edmondson Village.

The tension and anxiety was thick as they entered the building and headed to JR's spacious office in the back of the facility. Once inside his office, they all took seats around the oval shaped conference table, adorned with custom made Italian leather chairs and European furniture.

JR took his seat at the head of the table with Demon at his side. It was show time. JR was about to go into beast mode.

"What's poppin' fellas? I'm glad you all decided to show up for this meeting. That means a lot to me. I know that time is money, so I'ma just get right down to it. Since my mentor, Polo, died, the streets have been hurting without that good shit he was hittin' everybody off with on the low low. The fiends ain't satisfied with the bullshit dope that's out there, and ain't nobody making no real money, but my team. As the heir to his throne, of course, I inherited his connections as well. That's why I brought you all here to make you an offer and it would be wise for you not to refuse," JR said in a mild but subtly threatening tone.

All of the bosses wore a tight look on their faces.

"Spit it out what you gotta say, young blood. We ain't got all day. Make it plain, make it plain," Big Slim barked.

Dressed in a silk pants suit, Big Slim was an OG in the game that came up with Polo and Nigel back in the days. Over the years, he had done several small stretches in jail, but nothing major. He kept a low profile and stacked his money quietly. He didn't like the flashy lifestyle of the younger hustlers today, and detested having to do business with them. He was what you would call a gentleman's gangster. He lived a low-key lifestyle but everybody in his neighborhood knew who he was. He was the man to go to if somebody was about to be evicted or have their gas and electric shut off. He never asked for the money back when he did those kinds of charitable deeds. He believed that it was his way of giving back to the streets that he had hurt so much from filling the neighborhood with dope. He was also a silent force to be reckoned with, if tested.

Truth be told, he didn't trust JR. He didn't sense

any remorse or sincere mourning over Polo's death in his voice when he mentioned him. Something about JR's entire demeanor didn't sit right in his gut, but he couldn't put his finger on what exactly it was about him that irked him so. For now, he planned to play it cool until more was revealed.

"JR, we know you on some bullshit. I see you sitting back in that chair looking at us like we work for you or some shit. I'ma boss just like you," Prince chimed in. Prince was a pretty boy, just as his name suggested. He had the wavy hair, light brown eyes, and cocky arrogance that the ladies loved. He was the kind of hustler whose greatest vice was tricking his money away on broads. He had a good talk game, but his heart was soft as cotton when tested. He was definitely the weakest link in the room.

"Ok, first of all, y'all are in my motherfucking house, so show some respect. I recognize that we are all bosses, but I'm the boss of all bosses in this bitch. To make it plain, y'all need this work I got, if you wanna hold on to them corners you got now. I'm willing to let you all eat for a fair price for this product. I'm willing to hit you off with them birds at the same price that Polo was getting them to you for, because I'ma fair man," JR stated bluntly.

"Now that's what I'm talking about! Let's all get paid!" Prince chimed in.

"That sounds good to me," Fat Chris cut in.

His name was an accurate assessment of his body weight. Standing only five feet and two inches, he was at least three hundred pounds of pure blubber. He was the poster boy for obesity, diabetes, and high blood pressure, all rolled into one hefty sized little man. However, despite his weight issues, Fat Chris was smart and ran a highly organized crew of hustlers. He was serious about his money, and made every penny count for something. He was what one called a ghetto entrepreneur. He used his finances to open several businesses in his neighborhood.

"Hold up, don't go getting all excited just yet. It's seems as though young blood got something else on his mind," Big Slim reasoned. He had a good mind for reading people's ulterior motives. He tried to feel JR out to get a gauge on his thoughts. He had a feeling that JR was about to throw some salt in the game.

"Good observation, Slim. I always knew you were a smart dude. He's right about there being something else. In exchange for my generosity in extending my quality product to you, I'm expecting a ten stack a month kickback from each of you," JR stated with conviction and not a slight hint of flexibility for negotiation.

"Ten more stacks a month? Nigga is you crazy? You done lost your mind!" Money Marvin declared.

Money Marvin was a short, muscular cat who wore his hair in cornrows. He knew of JR well, because they came up in the game around the same time. He always hated how JR rose up so fast in the ranks with Polo, while he had to grind it out with the foot soldiers for so long before he got a chance to get caked up in his uncle Ice's organization.

"JR, you know that's highway robbery. Come on, bro, we all are just trying to eat out here just like you," Bop chimed in.

A slender brother with a calm demeanor, Bop didn't fit the stereotypical image of a drug dealer. He dressed like the preppy college kid that he was. Bop had a Bachelor's degree in Sociology from Morgan State University and was very intellectual. He sold drugs, but he also used the money he made to fund several community centers throughout the city. They were a great smokescreen for his illegal activities.

Bop attempted to be a calm voice of reason in the room. He'd always had a good relationship with JR, and there was mutual respect between them. They attended the same high school and were from the same neighborhood. He hoped that these factors would give him favor with JR, but JR was on his grown man shit. This was a new day, and he was a new man. He had the wind beneath him and felt firm and strong in his position to make such unreasonable demands.

"Well, fellas, the choice is yours. You have two choices. Either you can take my terms and we can all shake hands like businessmen, or I can simply wipe the floor with all of your asses and just take over your territories one by one. I think you all know I got the muscle and the product to make that happen. Don't test my hand. I'ma step out the room for a minute and let you talk amongst yourselves. Let it all marinate in ya minds for a few. When I come back, I'm expecting an answer," JR stated firmly.

He got up from his chair and walked out of the room. JR didn't want to go to war, but he was prepared to if need be. He had the muscle to carry out his threat, but he didn't want to resort to that unless it was absolutely necessary. Getting money with little to no bloodshed was the preferred option. He listened outside of the door and could hear the grumblings and complaints amongst them. After a while, the loud voices turned to calm conversation. He gave them another ten minutes to talk before he re-entered the room.

"Well, gentlemen, what did you decide?" JR asked directly.

"You say that like we have a choice in the matter, young blood. It's like you're asking a dying man does he wanna live or dangling a steak in Fat Chris' face and asking him if he wanna eat? You know damn well we're trying to get down. Money is king in my world, baby. You got yourself a deal," Big Slim responded.

The other bosses begrudgingly nodded their heads in agreement.

"Now that's what I wanted to hear. Now let me it break it down to y'all how this is gonna go," JR said as he laid out the plan.

He broke down how the work would be distributed and who would be responsible for collecting his money. They all listened attentively to his instructions. He had them all right where he wanted them. He also knew that he was playing a dangerous game. He had just made himself a marked man in the streets. Whenever someone had the kind of money and power that he would soon yield, it was inevitable that some hungry soul sat in the background plotting on a major come up. He accepted this reality and knew that he had to stay on his A game and not get caught slipping. Pretty soon, he would have so much money that he could use it for toilet paper to wipe his ass. Just like that, JR went from underboss to boss of all bosses. Now that he was crowned The King, his life would never be the same.

1

JR sat silently in his new cream-colored Bentley Azzure, staring into space. He took a pull off the perfectly rolled blunt that hung from his mouth. The sweet scent of the herbs seemed to calm his uneasy soul as it pierced the membranes of his nostrils. His lungs sucked in the smoke, and the weed did its job, as it relaxed his nerves temporarily. He needed to be high to confront the demons that had haunted him and constantly invaded his thoughts around this same time every year. Today was the anniversary of the death of his best friend and road dawg, Raynard. Every year, he made plans to take a trip out to King's Park Memorial cemetery in Randallstown to pay his respects to his fallen comrade, but he never followed through with his plans.

The deeply rooted pain from Raynard's murder never seemed to ease its hold on him, no matter how much time had passed. Death by gunfire was not an unusual occurrence for JR to see in his line of work. However, given his close relationship with Raynard, it hit him harder than any of the other hundreds of drug related murders that took place on the streets of Baltimore every year. With all of the good things going on in his life, this was the one dark patch that ate away at his soul. Not making the trip out to the cemetery was his way of being in denial of the fact that he would never see his homey again. Death was a permanent state of being, regardless of who you were.

JR had many conversations with his father about how much Raynard's death weighed heavily on him. He had grown to feel comfortable enough with Nigel to confide in him about his dilemma. They had developed the sincere father and son relationship that he had always craved. It felt good for him to have Nigel around as a confidant in his times of need. He knew that his father could relate to his pain because he came up in the streets himself, and had lost so many of his own partners the same way.

Nigel advised him that he had to learn acceptance and let go of the burden of Raynard's memory. Acceptance was one of the key attributes Nigel had incorporated into his recovery process that not only applied to drug addiction, but to everyday life as well. It took a while for Nigel's advice to sink in, but JR was finally ready to free his soul. He had finally come to grips with the bitter reality that his brother and road dawg was gone forever, and he wanted to break free from the shackles of mental bondage. He chose today to be the day he would face his demons head on.

Unable to delay his journey any longer, JR stepped out of his car and proceeded to walk towards the area of the cemetery where Raynard was buried. The walk seemed like an eternity before he reached Raynard's headstone. He passed the corpses of many other fallen soldiers along the way, and wondered to himself if their loved ones were faced with the same type of intense feelings that he experienced. As he walked, he was filled with feelings of anxiety and lightheadedness. When he reached Raynard's burial plot, his eyes watered and blurred his vision. He was glad to be alone, because he made it a rule to never allow anyone to see him cry. He was a hard core G, and to cry was a sign of weakness for a boss. His tears were for his eyes only. Not even the love of his life, Rochelle, was allowed to see this side of him.

When Raynard died, a piece of JR died along with him. He was the closest thing to a brother that he had growing up. Not being blood related didn't weaken the bond between them. All of the years that his father wasn't in his life to guide him were filled up with him and Raynard earning their rights of passage to manhood out in the streets together putting in work. They went through everything together, from slinging G packs, smashing broads, getting locked up, and busting their guns back to back in the heat of battle. He hated that they had a falling out before he died, and that they never got a chance to reconcile their differences. That was the biggest regret in his young troubled life. The memory of getting that dreaded call about Raynard's death was stuck on repeat in his head. He wished he could flip back the hands of time to take back his actions that led to their falling out, but time stood still or went in reverse for no man.

As he reminisced on the good times that they had, JR cracked the bottle of Hennessy in his hand and proceeded to take man sized gulps to the head. He poured some on the ground, in hopes that it would seep through the dirt down to his homey so they could share a taste together like they had done so many times in the past. Feeling a buzz from the weed, the Henny only added to his semi-lucid state of mind. He proceeded to take shots to the head until the entire fifth of alcohol was gone. Fully intoxicated from the liquor and high off of the weed, he rumbled words from the heart in a cryptic conversation with the buried remains of his partner.

"What up, Ray? You know I miss you, dawg. I wish you were here with me gettin' some of this money. I got it coming in stacks tall as Shaq. Ya boy gettin' that Freeway Rick Ross money. I'm gettin' that Charles Cosby Cocaine Cowboy guap, homey! I done came up out here and now I'm livin' like a King. I'm doing it up big like we always said we would. All these suckas out here is hatin' on my shine. They wanna knock me off my throne, but you know ya boy ain't going out like that.

"I run these streets out here. I got that mansion with all the fly ass whips in the driveway. I married Rochelle, just like you always said I would. You knew she had her hooks in a player for life. Quentin and Savion are both getting big, dawg. Q's got it in his head that he's gonna be a running back in the NFL and shit, while Savion is the book worm. I can see him being a doctor one day. You know I ain't letting them come nowhere near this street life as long as I'm breathing. I want something different for them apart from this thing of ours. Ya girl, Latrice, man she on some wild shit. Shawty done lost her mind since you've been gone, fucking around with all these different niggas out here. I tried to reach out to her, but she ain't trying to hear shit. She doesn't even fuck with Rochelle anymore. She won't even let me see lil' Ray Ray. I go by his school every now and then to check on him, though. He's getting big, looking just like you, homey. Damn, I miss you, homey!" he cried out in pain. He pounded his hand on the headstone. The alcohol had him open and all up in his feelings.

He was down on his knees with his head pressed against Raynard's headstone. More tears fell from his eyes to the dirt and grass beneath his feet. He took his hand and wiped his face. When he looked up, his feelings of mourning were replaced with blind rage at the sight of Polo's headstone that was adjacent to Raynard's. Just as strongly as he felt love for Raynard, he had a similar intensity of hatred for his father, due to all the drama and pain he experienced as a result of Polo's grudge with Nigel. He loved Raynard like a brother, but he felt no regret about playing a major role in killing his father. He reasoned that Polo reserved his own seat in hell for all of the suffering that he caused him over some foolishness that he had nothing to do with at all. JR genuinely had love for Polo, and saw him as a father figure, only to find out that he was just a pawn in his twisted game of revenge. Overcome with rage, his liquid courage from the Henny led him to embark on another verbal tirade.

"Now ya pops, dawg, that motherfucker was a grimy son of a bitch. He was playing me from day one. That slimy bastard killed my moms, fucked my girl, and tried to get me to kill my Pops on his revenge shit. And I actually thought this motherfucker looked at me like a son, and us as brothers, when all along, he had some slick shit up his sleeve. I love you like we're blood, but to see that bastard put to sleep was some straight up street justice. I hate his ass like my grandmother hates the devil. You can't even get mad at me for that one, homey. If you were in my place, you woulda did the same thing and handled your business," he muttered.

JR looked up to the sky as if he were looking for Raynard to send a sign from heaven that he understood his pain.

As he glanced at Polo's last resting place, he felt a need to drive home further his hatred for him. He cleared his throat and hurled a big glob of spit at Polo's name that was engraved on the headstone. Taking it a step further, he unzipped his pants and proceeded to relieve his full bladder all over Polo's burial plot. He closed his eyes and felt a sense of relief once all of his waste materials were littered over

Polo's gravesite. He reached inside his jacket pocket, pulled out a freshly rolled blunt, and lit it, taking a pull straight to the head. Next, he placed it on the ground in front of Raynard's headstone and stomped out the flames. He left it there as a symbol and lasting memory of how they used to blaze up together. He took one last glance at his homey's final home on Earth and began his trek back to his whip.

He had accomplished what he set out to do. He could finally put the burden of Raynard's memory behind him and move on with his life. He could also let go of the hatred he had for Polo. His soul was now free from the heavy burden.

JR hopped inside his whip and cranked up the surround sound stereo system. He bobbed his head to the sounds of Kendrick Lamar's new CD as he dipped in and out traffic. His jam session was interrupted by an incoming call. He looked at the navigation screen and a smile came across his face. It was his six-year-old little brother, Malachi, on the line, calling from his father's phone. He loved spending time with him whenever he could get free to do so. That was his little man.

"Yeah, who's this on my phone?" JR asked in a deep baritone voice.

"JR, it's me Malachi. Why are you playing with me? You know my voice by now," Malachi replied as he giggled.

"Boy, you know I know it's you. Where's Pops?" JR asked jokingly.

"He's right here. We're waiting for you. You're taking too long. Are you on your way?" Malachi inquired.

"Yeah, I'ma be there in like an hour. I had to handle some business first. Stop questioning me, shawty. I'm the big brother, remember that. Don't make me have to knock you out," JR said.

He needed the extra time to let the buzz of the weed and alcohol wear off some before he saw his father. He tried to never go around him high, because a lecture about recovery and saying no to drugs would then be inevitable. He took the bottle of Listerine from his center console and downed the whole thing in an attempt to cover up the smell of alcohol on his breath. Next, he doused himself in cologne to hide the scent of weed.

"I might be little, but you don't want it with me, big bro," Malachi uttered in response. To be so young, he already had swagger and bravado. He was truly a Hawkins man.

"I don't want no problems with you, lil' Man. I surrender. I'll see you when I get there," JR replied submissively. He hit the "End call" button on the navigation screen to disconnect the call.

Every other Saturday afternoon, the Hawkins men would get together to eat either lunch or dinner. Usually, he brought Savion and Quentin with him, but he didn't have time today to go home to pick them up. This ritual was his way of bonding with his father, and for them all to spend time together as a family. JR had gotten to know his father very well since he came back in his life, and he cherished their relationship. Even though Nigel didn't approve of his lifestyle, they both agreed to not let it get in the way of their having a relationship. Too much time had passed while Nigel was in jail, for that to be a barrier. Nigel simply let JR know that he would always be there for him, if he ever decided that he had enough of the game.

The time they spent together gave JR a much needed break from his every day non-stop action paced life of ripping and running in the streets and running a criminal enterprise. It kept him sane and able to have some form of balance in his life, despite the constant threat of danger that lurked around the corner.

He weaved through traffic with the top down in his luxury toy that had cost him a little over four hundred grand in cash. Along with the pleasure, there would always be a heavy dose of pain. This was the life he chose as a Boss, and he accepted it like a soldier. He wouldn't have it any other way.

2

Nigel sat behind his desk in the office of Hawkins Realty, Inc., which was located in West Baltimore near Druid Hill Park. He enjoyed the view of the lake from the window behind his desk. The sweet smell of freedom and serenity permeated the air. He was drug-free, no longer on parole, happily married to the love of his life, Nicole, and had a chance to do things right this time as a father with his young son, Malachi. He also had JR back in his world after such a long hiatus. In addition to the strong bond he shared with JR and Malachi, he had also developed a good relationship with his stepdaughter, Crystal, who was now a freshman at Georgetown University. The insanity of his thoughts while in a drug induced state were far behind him. He was a different man today, with a new outlook on life.

Instead of teaching Malachi how to become a thug and menace to society, like he did with JR, he planned to instill in him all of the necessary values to become a responsible and well respected man. He gave him the name, Malachi, because he wanted him to have a name with a significant meaning and purpose. Malachi, in Hebrew, meant "Messenger of God" and that is exactly what he was to Nigel. He was his guardian angel, and a perfect reflection of the best side of him. Malachi's birth was akin to Nigel's rebirth as a new man and as a father. He envisioned him one day as a politician or the CEO of a powerful corporation. Whatever he chose to do, Nigel was dead set on him breaking the generational curse of crime and debauchery that was started by his father and carried on by himself and JR.

Nigel started the real estate company three years ago with the seed money JR gave him to get on his feet after he lost his last job as a construction worker. Initially, he didn't want to take the money from JR because he was sincere about distancing himself totally from that way of life and all of its financial benefits. However, after not being able to hold on to a steady job that afforded him a chance to make enough money to provide the kind of life that he wanted to for his family, he reconsidered his options. He took the money that JR gave him and bought two abandoned homes in West Baltimore for under ten grand. He used the rest of the money to rehab them and make them suitable for renting out for Section 8 housing. In no time at all, he had built good enough credit and generated enough revenue to buy several more homes from homeowners that had fallen behind on their mortgage and were desperate to get out of their dire financial situation.

Once he bought the homes, he would quickly resell them for nothing less than double his investment. Business had become so profitable for him, that Nicole decided to quit her job as a parole agent and get her real estate sales license. With her by his side as his business partner, they were successful in making Hawkins Realty a legitimate high stakes player in the Baltimore real estate market. He had hired three other real estate agents to join his staff as a part of his plans to expand operations. Nigel Hawkins, the dope fiend junkie, ex-convict, and drug dealing thug was now a responsible father, husband,

and legitimate real estate mogul. He was a widely respected member of the African American business community. He attributed his good fortune to his faith in God and his choice to live an upright life.

His faith in religion was shaken when he found out about the double life of his dope peddling former pastor, Rev. Johnnie Mitchell. However, his living testimony of having risen from the ashes of having nothing, to now having blessings in abundance made him reconsider abandoning his faith. His mother's stern persistence and Nicole's positive influence also helped him to understand that Rev. Mitchell, and not the religion of Christianity, had fallen short in its duty to provide divine guidance to the people of God.

When he saw on the news a while back that Rev. Mitchell was arrested on RICO charges for running a criminal enterprise through his church and sentenced to 25 years to life, Nigel got a clearer picture of just how the universal law of karma never slept. His faith in his higher power was restored and renewed. He found a new church home at the Temple of New Life AME Church that was run by a true man of God, the Reverend Richard F. Reid. He made sure that he attended church services every Sunday with his mother, Nicole, and Malachi in tow.

Nicole stood by his side through his daily battle with his sobriety. She attended NA meetings with him on a regular basis to give him emotional support. Even though he had been clean now for over six years, every now and then, Nigel felt the urge to use. The habits of an addict die hard, no matter how much clean time he had, but Nicole was right there like a watchdog to snap him back into reality. She, of course, had Mrs. Hawkins' full support to keep her son on the straight and narrow path. With these two women in his corner to fight his battle with him, Nigel grew to understand that he had a responsibility to become a better man than he was in the past. Looking at what he had accomplished in such a short time, it was clear that he stepped up to the plate in a major way to handle his business like a man. He was a living testament to the power of redemption.

Nigel smiled as he watched Malachi run back and forth through his office as he played his with toys. His non-stop level of energy was amazing. He got himself a gym membership to stay in shape, so that he would be able to keep up with him. He brought him into the office with him on Saturdays because that was usually a light day with not much going on. Nigel normally just finished leftover paperwork from earlier in the week that needed to be glanced over one last time before he closed a sale. He thanked God every day for delivering him from his evil ways and for never losing faith in his ability to get back on the path of righteousness that was ordained for him from birth.

If he needed a reminder of just how blessed he was, all he had to do daily was look at the picture of his beautiful wife, Nicole, and his son, Malachi, that rested on his desk. They were living proof that all of his blessings were in fact real, and divinely ordained for him to have. He looked up from his work to see that Malachi had run smack dead into the end table and hurt his knee. Malachi winced for a second and got right back to playing. Children were resilient in that way.

"Be careful, son. Don't hurt yourself now. You need to slow down before you run into something else. Daddy doesn't want to have to take you to the hospital. You know your mother would kill me," Nigel stated.

"Okay, Daddy, but you know I'm a big boy now. I can handle a little pain, even though Mommy thinks

I'm still a baby," he replied innocently. He ran back and forth across the plush carpet playing with his toy cars.

"Boy, you are always gonna be her baby, no matter how old you are," Nigel replied.

Nigel had to laugh at his son's tough guy routine. Some of the things that came out of his mouth would at times make Nigel stop in his tracks. He didn't know where he learned some of the stuff he spit out. Whenever he had a bad day, all he had to do to relieve his mind was to recall something funny that Malachi had said to him out of the blue. As he glanced over some papers on his desk, he was interrupted when his office door suddenly opened.

"Baby, can you look this paperwork over for me so that I can close this deal out?" Nicole requested. She planted a light kiss on Nigel's cheek that brought a smile to his face.

Nicole usually didn't come into the office on the weekends with Nigel, but today was different. She was in the middle of a huge home sale to a young couple, Damon and Paulette Wedstone, which could possibly be her biggest sale yet. The Wedstones were newlyweds and looking to buy their first home. Their mid hundred grand combined incomes made them eligible to purchase whatever home they wanted. Nicole used her charm and witty personality to sell them on one of their properties, and they were able to get financing from Damon's credit union. Once the deal went through, Nicole would get a healthy sales commission. A trip to the outlet mall in Hagerstown would have to be arranged with her daughter in law, Rochelle, to spend some of her hard-earned money.

As Nigel perused the documents, Nicole occupied herself briefly by playing with Malachi. She chased behind him inside of Nigel's massive executive suite.

When she caught him, she tickled his ribs. Malachi laughed until his belly began to ache. Nicole genuinely loved Nigel and the life they shared together. Even though they met under dubious terms, with her being his parole agent, somehow they managed to form an unbreakable bond that defied the odds.

During the time she worked as a parole agent, there were rumors circulating around the office about her relationship with Nigel, because of how frequently he came into the office to see her, but no one could prove a damn thing. Truth be told, she didn't care what people thought about their relationship. All she knew was that she had a good man who loved her infinitely. The nice four bedroom, three bathroom home and sexy Mercedes E350 that she was able to afford, thanks to their thriving business were added perks that solidified in her mind that she did the right thing, giving into temptation with Nigel Hawkins. A few times, she ran into old coworkers who would sneer when they saw her with Nigel, but she just laughed in their faces. They could hate all they wanted because she was happy with her man.

When she looked over at Nigel, she admired how much he had grown as a man from the time he first entered her office as a parolee fresh out of the penitentiary. Her feelings of insecurity that she used to have with men were non-existent now that she had found her soul mate. Throughout the course of her relationship with Nigel, Nicole also had developed a close bond with Rochelle. It wasn't like a mother and daughter type of thing, because they were so close in age, but it was more of a sisterly connection. They would get together with the kids on the weekends and go shopping or just for some girl time like a day of pampering at a day spa. They also confided in each other whenever they needed to vent about the

Hawkins men and their ways. They had each other's back when it was needed.

Nicole's relationship with JR was nowhere near as close. Even though she accepted JR into her life, she also had her reservations about his illegal activities. She knew that Nigel carried around a great deal of guilt and feelings of responsibility for turning his son on to the street life, but she didn't want him to be caught up in JR's dangerous lifestyle, trying to save him. She knew that she couldn't tell him not to have a relationship with his son, because that wasn't going to happen. However, she also wanted to hold on to the life they had built together with Malachi.

She saw JR as a potential threat to their happy home, because she envisioned that one day, JR would get himself into some trouble with the law and Nigel would feel obligated to help him out of it without regard for the impact it may have on her and Malachi. She saw this type of scenario play out many times in her years as a parole agent, and it usually never ended in a good way. Initially, she and Nigel would argue about this issue, before she relented and decided to let things run their natural course. At the same time, she kept her eyes and ears open to make sure that none of JR's mess became their mess.

"Well honey, everything looks to be in order. All we have to do now is to set up a closing date and we can wrap this deal up. How are you coming along with the sale of that four bedroom house out in Ellicott City?" he asked.

"I have a few people that wanna see the property scheduled for next week, so I'll see how it goes," she replied.

"That's what I'm talking about! Well, you can wrap this up because me and the lil' man are about to be on our way, once JR gets here," Nigel stated.

No sooner than the words left his mouth, JR rang the bell at the front door. Nigel hit the buzzer to let him in. JR walked past Nicole's office and noticed the modest looking White couple seated in there alone. He nodded his head to say hello to the Wedstones. They were taken back by the sight of this young Black male dressed in baggy jeans and a hooded sweatshirt inside of such a prestigious looking real estate office. JR cracked a smile. He sensed the fear that his presence instilled in the harmless looking Caucasian couple. They looked like Satan himself stood before them. The image of the urban Black male was obviously foreign to them, other than what they saw in the media.

"Y'all don't have to worry. I'm not here to rob the place, so relax. I'm Nigel's son, JR. I'ma business man too," JR said with a grin.

The Wedstones didn't know what to say. They sat there speechless and feeling uncomfortable. They saw no connection between the rugged looking character before them and Nigel, who always dressed professionally in a shirt and tie. He must be adopted they reasoned to themselves.

Nigel heard JR's voice in the hallway and walked towards Nicole's office. He sensed that his clients might be caught off guard by his son's persona, and hastily made his way down to intercede. Nicole followed closely behind him. Malachi heard his big brother's voice and couldn't wait to see him.

"How are you doing, Mr. and Mrs. Wedstone? This is my son, Nigel Jr. Please excuse him. He likes to joke around a lot. I'm glad that we could be of service to you in helping you purchase your first home. I know you are both excited!" Nigel exclaimed.

He shot JR a look as if to say, 'don't scare my clients away.' He could smell through his cologne bath, the stench of marijuana and alcohol on him, but refused to let his disappointment show. Malachi grabbed JR's leg and playfully punched him in the thigh. JR picked him up and tossed him over his shoulder. Malachi couldn't stop laughing.

"No problem at all. Yes, we are excited about the purchase. We can't wait to move into our new home!" Mr. Wedstone replied.

"Great. Well, my wife will take good care of you from here on out. If you have any questions, feel free to contact me," he stated. He shook hands with Mr. Wedstone and exited Nicole's office. He dragged JR along with him. Nicole stayed behind to finish her business.

"Damn, Pops, you sound just like a white man with all of that proper talk. You really got it going on with this real estate thing. You used my money wisely," JR stated. He was genuinely impressed with his father's progress in life. He also wanted to remind him his dirty money helped put him there.

"I do what I gotta do to make the deals work, son. I'm a business man," Nigel replied.

"Well, Mr. Big Shot business man, where are we eating at today?" JR asked.

"I was thinking that we could go to Longhorn's Steakhouse. I'm in the mood for one of them big ole eighteen ounce porterhouse steaks," he replied.

"That works for me. What about you lil' man? What do you want to eat? You're da real boss around here," JR joked.

"I'm hungry as a hostage. It doesn't matter to me. JR, can I come over your house tonight so I can play with Savion and Quentin?" Malachi replied. JR's boys were a few years older than Malachi, but they both loved hanging out with their younger uncle.

"Man, of course you can come over. After we eat,

I'ma take you by the crib. They got some new games for the PlayStation 3 that I know you wanna play," JR replied.

Malachi was elated.

"Well, let's get outta here!" Nigel said.

The three Hawkins men exited Nigel's office. On the way out, Nigel motioned to Nicole to indicate that they were headed out and she would have to close up the office alone. When they stepped out of the office door, Nigel was thrown back by what he saw. This was the first time he had set his eyes upon JR's new ride. The Bentley Azzure was truly a sight to behold. The four hundred grand that it cost was also an attention grabber. Nigel shook his head in disapproval as they got in the car.

"Man, this car is sweet!" Malachi declared as he jumped in the back seat. He ran his little hand across the fine leather trim. He was equally fascinated when JR started the car and the dashboard illuminated. All of the fancy gadgets had him mesmerized.

"Thanks, lil' man. You go to school, get good grades, and become a doctor or lawyer. You'll be able to buy yourself one too someday," JR said proudly.

"Is that what you do JR? Are you a doctor or lawyer?" Malachi asked.

Nigel turned towards him, eager to hear his response.

"Nah, bro, I'm a businessman, just like Daddy. I sell merchandise and people buy a lot of it, to make me a lot of money," JR replied coyly. He winked at Nigel, but Nigel was hardly amused.

At times like this, Nigel felt a deep sense of regret and guilt that he had introduced JR to the street life at around the same age that Malachi was currently. He felt that he was the reason JR was so messed up in the head and addicted to the rush of the game that he couldn't let it go. Even though he didn't want to admit it, sometimes JR felt jealous and cheated by the way Nigel treated Malachi, compared to how he used to treat him when he was his age. His father was warm, loving, and compassionate with his little brother, while he was cold hearted and raw with him coming up. He knew that his father was a different man today, but that still couldn't totally take away the emotional scars that his childhood had left behind. Besides, he loved them both too much to let his emotional baggage impact their relationship, so he never let his subconscious thoughts surface.

"What kind of merchandise?" Malachi asked innocently. Before JR could respond, Nigel cut in to nip the conversation in the bud.

"Boy, stop asking so many questions," Nigel said sternly.

The seriousness of his father's tone made Malachi not want an answer to his question. He went back into his own little world, admiring the fancy buttons around the car interior. JR turned up the radio and Malachi started bopping his little head back and forth to the sounds of the music. Nigel shot JR a dirty look as he drove down the road.

"Pops, what's wrong? Why are you tripping today?" JR asked.

"I'm not trippin', son. Sometimes I wish you would think about things before you do them. I think you wanna get knocked off. You're a young black male riding around in this car that cost as much as a mansion, and you're asking me what's wrong? If you have to ask, then I guess I didn't teach you well," Nigel replied coldly. He was clearly disappointed.

Even though he didn't approve of JR's lifestyle, he at least hoped that he would be smart about how he handled his business. Nigel had taught JR to not be so flashy and flamboyant in displaying the fruits of his drug money. It was the easiest way to get jammed up by the law. Judging by the platinum chain dangling from his neck and the platinum rings on his pinky and index fingers, JR had obviously forgotten about those lessons.

"Be cool, Pops. I got this. I wanted to treat myself to something nice, so I got this ride. Besides, I own this city. I got the police department on my payroll. If one of these lil' rent a cops run up on me, all it will take is one phone call from my attorney to the Police Chief and he'll be working traffic detail. My arm is that strong right now. Your son is something of a big deal out here in these streets," he replied cockily.

As his power and influence in the streets grew, so too did JR's ego. No doubt about it, he was the man in the streets and had no problem letting it be known. However, in the drug game, that was subject to change at any moment, given the right set of unfortunate circumstances. Any drug kingpin was just one snitch or murder away from his world being flipped upside down.

"I hear you, Mr. Big Shot. Just know that nobody is invincible, but God," he shot back.

"Aww, here you go with the God talk. I know what I'm doing. I handle my business smartly out here. I ain't gonna make the same mistakes you made, dippin' into my own product. I'm too smart for that, Pops," JR stated to reiterate his point. He wished he could take those words back but the damage was already done.

"Watch it boy, be careful what you say out ya mouth. I know I used to get high and messed up things in the past, but this old junkie is still your father!" Nigel said angrily.

Nigel might've been a reformed man, but he

didn't take too kindly to being insulted by his own son. He wasn't too holy to administer an ass whipping on demand.

"I'm sorry, Pops. I ain't mean to say it like that. You know I'm proud of you and how you got your life together, and all. You should never doubt that. I meant to say that you don't have to worry about me, is all. I'm my own man. I can carry my own weight. I know what I'm doing. I know you don't approve of what I do, but it's my choice. Now, let's just go get something to eat and have a good time," JR stated. He knew he had just shot a low blow at his father and wanted to make up for it as best he could.

Nigel didn't respond. He just laid back against the plush headrest. He said a silent prayer that God would open up JR's eyes before it was too late. His arrogance had him blind to all of the unforeseen traps that lie in wait to ensnare him. He knew from experience, that being overly confident and letting power go to your head was the easiest to get caught slipping out in the streets. JR was high off the power of his wealth, the same way he used to be off cocaine. The adrenaline rush was damn near the same, with consequences equally as deadly.

JR was so caught up in the hype of himself, that he never saw the unmarked car that had followed him from the cemetery, snapping pictures of his every move. The unseen enemy was always the worst to deal with, because you never saw them coming.

3

I'm getting too old for the games and the lies! Rochelle declared as she pushed the "End call" button on her cell phone. She walked down the hallway of the hospital with a look on her face that said, 'don't F with me today.' She was beyond pissed off. She had called JR at least twenty times already, and each time, his phone went straight to voicemail. She needed him to pick the boys up from school because she had to work late, but he didn't seem to give enough of a damn to answer his phone. If he didn't answer his phone, it usually meant that he was into something or someone that he had no business being involved with from the jump.

"Rochelle, is everything okay? You look a little upset. Is there anything that I can do to help?" Jerry asked.

Jerry happened to be walking by her in the opposite direction and couldn't help being curious when he observed her as she mumbled several expletives to herself. He could see that something was wrong. Being a friend, he had no choice but to offer his assistance.

"No, I'm fine, but thanks for asking, Jerry," she replied.

"Are you sure? I meant it when I said if there is anything that you need, I'm always here for you. If you need somebody to talk to or just to listen," he stated with sincerity.

"Nah, I'm good. It's nothing I can't handle. It's just a little man trouble, is all it is. You're so sweet and thoughtful. You're good peeps, Jerry," she replied. Her anger briefly subsided and she cracked a slight smile.

While JR was busy becoming the king of the Baltimore underworld, Rochelle wasn't the type of chick to just sit home on her butt and do nothing. With JR's blessing, she had enrolled in classes at Coppin State University and had managed to obtain her Bachelor's degree in Nursing. Initially, she was a Business Management major, but she changed her mind and decided instead to pursue her passion for helping people. After graduating, she landed a job as an RN at the University of Maryland Medical Center's R. Adams Cowley Shock Trauma Center. She never had a dull day on the job, because the trauma center stayed filled with clients who suffered head trauma injuries, gunshot wounds, and a host of other life threatening medical complications.

She loved to help people, and she was good at what she did. Plus, her seventy-five grand a year salary was nothing to sneeze at for a young black girl from the hood. Even though she had a man that was filthy rich and gave her whatever she wanted, it made her feel good about herself to have her own money as well. With or without JR, she could provide financially for her two children.

Jerry was a dark skinned with brother with a medium build. He was about an inch or two taller than Rochelle. He wasn't what you would describe as a sex symbol type of guy that women drooled over, but he wasn't ugly either. His kind and sincere demeanor made him popular amongst the female nurses. They looked at him like a brother or good friend. Jerry had a crush on Rochelle since the first day he saw her, when she came in for her initial interview for the job. He was captivated by her bright smile and the dazzling aura that she exuded when he walked past her, sitting outside of the human resources office.

A nurse himself, he was very eager for an opportunity to get to know this fine looking sister a little better. When he found out that she would be working on the same shift as him, he laid out a plan in his head on how he was going to hook her. However, his plans were dashed when he saw the dazzling six-carat platinum diamond ring on her finger. That made her off limits to him. He had to settle for friendship as a consolation prize.

"Well, JR better get it together. Any man that that doesn't know how to keep a smile on your beautiful face is a damn fool. And you can tell him I said that," Jerry said boldly.

"I sure will let him know, buddy," Rochelle replied as Jerry walked away. She knew Jerry was no more of threat to do any harm to JR than a newborn baby. Nonetheless, she thought his desire to defend her honor was a cute gesture.

Since she couldn't reach JR, Rochelle decided to give Nicole a call. If she wasn't busy, she knew that she would be more than happy to pick up Quentin and Savion from school for her. Despite her mixed feelings about JR, she loved those boys with all of her heart and would do anything in the world for them. She spoiled them almost as much as she spoiled Malachi. Whenever she took him shopping for clothes or toys, somehow things always seemed to land in her shopping cart for both Quentin and Savion. To them, she was the best grandmother in the world.

When Rochelle dialed her number, Nicole answered on the fourth ring.

"Hey, daughter in law, how are you doing today?" Nicole asked cheerfully.

"I'm good, I guess," she said in a wishy-washy tone.

"Oh, lawd, what's going on, girl? Tell me all about it. What did my stepson do now?" Nicole asked as if she had heard this story before. Even if she did, she would still listen to it once again, because she genuinely cared for Rochelle.

"You know me too well. He's not answering his phone and I need him to pick the boys up because I have to work late. I know he's probably with some little tramp, but, of course, he'll lie and say he was somewhere at a meeting or taking care of business," Rochelle said, sounding dejected.

Rochelle loved JR more than one woman should love any man. She knew that she was dead wrong to have slept with Polo years ago, but she did everything in her power since that time to make up for her mishap. JR threw it up in her face many times when she caught him out with another woman. At first, because of her guilt, she felt that she deserved to be treated badly. However, that notion wore off over time. She used to accept all of the shopping sprees or new cars as makeup gifts, and just forgave him with little resistance whenever he tried to make up for stepping out on her. However, his womanizing had started to wear on her emotionally. She knew that she deserved to be treated better. She was an intelligent and educated professional black woman. She had made a successful story of her life, despite her mother's drug addiction and her rough childhood. There was no doubt that she was a strong black woman. However, she was still insanely weak for her man, and haunted by a deep inner fear of being alone.

Her mother had died two years prior from

endocarditis, which was a result of her many years of drug abuse. She had no other living family members in Baltimore with whom she had a relationship growing up. Her old best friend, Latrice, was no longer around because she was still running wild in the streets doing her own thing. She was happy when Nicole came around. She admired her and how she took charge in the relationship with Nigel. She remembered how she used to have a similar hold on JR when they were younger, and how it had changed slowly over the years. She looked forward to Nicole's many words of encouragement and good advice whenever they got together. One day, she planned to put it all into practice for herself in being more firm in her position when dealing with JR and his lack of consideration and respect for her feelings.

"Shoot, I wish Nigel would be out with some other woman. He thinks that he needs Viagra now to get his thing up, he'll need more than that once I cut it off!" Nicole said jokingly. On the real, she was dead serious. Nicole did not play games when it came to her heart, a fact that Nigel knew very well. Rochelle had to muffle her laughter because she was still at work and didn't want anyone in the hospital to hear her.

"Nicole, you are so crazy. My father in law taking Viagra is little bit too much info for me. Yuck! I know you're right, though. I deserve better. I do. On another note, can you get the boys for me if it's not too much of a hassle?" Rochelle asked.

"Of course I can. You know it's never a problem for me to get my grandkids. I'll take them over to see Mama Hawkins. It'll make her day," Nicole replied.

"Thanks, Nicole. I appreciate you," Rochelle stated sincerely.

"Girl, it's nothing. One more thing before I go. A man will only treat you how you allow him to treat you. Stand your ground with JR and put your foot down. You're his wife, not some damn tramp in the street. Remember that. Now get your butt back to work," she preached.

They said their goodbyes. Rochelle ended her break and got back to work.

Nicole loved being there for Rochelle, because she could relate to where she was in life. She never judged her because she used to be her before she met Nigel. She used to be the insecure woman going through dead end relationship after relationship, and never feeling that she was good enough to receive the kind of love she deserved. Falling in love with Nigel was the best thing that happened in her life. The way that he went all out to gain her love and approval enabled her to truly know her worth as a woman and set the bar high for how she expected to be treated by a man. Now she had to get Rochelle to see things in the same light.

Seeing how JR treated Rochelle, and the fact he was still caught up in the streets made her dislike for him grow. She didn't doubt that he loved Rochelle and the kids in his own way, but he was also a danger to them because of his lifestyle. She felt uneasy, at times, when Malachi would spend the night over JR's house. The only reason that she allowed him to stay over there was to keep the peace and to avoid an argument with Nigel. He wanted his sons to have a good relationship, and for her to stand in the way of that would have presented a problem. Even though he was Nigel's first-born child, she would be damned if JR would ever become a problem in their lives to the extent that Nigel would have to choose between him and her. That was a bridge she hoped to never cross.

4

JR's phone rang for the umpteenth time. He knew it was Rochelle. She did this all the time, whenever he left the house. It was the same routine, with her wanting to know where he was, and her threatening to leave if he didn't get back home right away. He paid her threats no mind, because he knew she wasn't going anywhere. He had that kitten locked down for life. Besides, she was too in love with the lavish lifestyle that she was able to live at his expense to ever let it go.

No other man could fill JR's shoes. He was her anything and everything. He was her king and she was his queen. Their two sons were a symbol of the best of both of them. They both took turns throughout their relationship, doing their share of dirt, but they would always wind up back together. Their bond was unexplainable and unbreakable. Nothing that Rochelle wanted had a price tag on it that JR wouldn't pay, in order to appease her desires. She was spoiled to death by her king. Good or bad, they were both in this relationship for life.

Rochelle always assumed that when he was gone for long periods of time that he was with another woman. In the past, she might have been right because JR had his share of side chicks that she had to deal with through the years. However, lately, chasing women was hardly on JR's mind. He was focused on getting money. He spent all of his time trying to figure out new ways to get more and more. He had his hands in so many different business ventures that sometimes it was hard for him to keep track of his financial empire.

Outside of the car wash, he owned the hottest nightclub in town, called the Money Kings Bar and Lounge. These two businesses were the only legitimate ones that he had in his name. A few years back, he was a in a bad car accident and he almost died. He suffered several physical injuries, in addition to his Lincoln Navigator being totaled. He received a cash settlement of over one hundred grand as compensation, thanks to some shrewd legal maneuvering by his attorney. The settlement was enough money for him to use as legitimate startup capital to open the car wash and nightclub.

The Money Kings Bar and Lounge was the central hub of his empire. He handled most of his business dealings inside of his lavish office in the upstairs area of the club. It was his biggest legal moneymaker, and where he and his top soldiers hung out to parlay on the weekends. He had a full sized two-bedroom apartment built into the upstairs area. That was his little getaway spot when he wanted to take one of his sidepieces for a quick romp in the sack. The club itself was the most state of the art nightclub on the East coast.

JR also invested in a soul food restaurant called the Soul Connection. He owned several rental and commercial properties and office buildings throughout the city. All of his other businesses were set up by his corporate attorney, Irwin Goldstein, in the names of different dummy corporations, so that the money could never be traced back to him. His real estate acquisitions were established in the same manner. He also provided the seed money for several barbershops and hair salons, scattered throughout the city, and remained a silent partner along with the shop's recognized owner. JR even financed the career of a hot local rapper named Hostile, in hopes that he would blow up and become a star one day.

JR wasn't just another ignorant drug dealer without vision, who planned to blow every penny he made in the streets. He had a vision for financial security and a diversified portfolio of profitable investments that he set up to maintain his boss lifestyle until the day he died. His sons and their offspring would be taken care of as well.

To be able to ensure a firm financial foundation for all of his business ventures, he had to make sure that the streets kept him well fed. JR wanted payment in full for every dollar that he was owed by anybody that copped work from him. Taking shorts was unacceptable in his position as the top dawg in the drug game. It could cost you your life to test his sincerity about his paper. Prince was foolish enough to test his hand. He had to learn the hard way not to play around with JR's money.

Prince had one day decided to grow a sack of balls and reach the conclusion that the ten stacks a month tax that JR required the other bosses to pay in order to be able to sell his dope was unreasonable. Somebody had gassed his head up to the point that he felt he was beyond JR's reach. One day, when JR sent Diggy to collect the money, he refused to pay. JR took this as blatant disrespect and ordered Demon to inflict any harsh punishment he chose upon him, with his blessing.

The consequence for his actions was that Prince died a slow brutal death at the hands of Demon, after being tortured for hours in countless ungodly ways.

After word hit the streets about his death, JR didn't have to worry about any form of rebellion from any of the other bosses. The message he sent was swift, direct, and clear—fuck with JR's bread and it's off with ya head.

Today, JR didn't have time to answer Rochelle's calls because he had urgent business that he needed to address. JR had received a call from his Colombian supplier, Julio, summoning him to New York for a sit down meeting with his council. Julio demanded that they meet today, right away. JR would have been a fool to say no to this request. He might be viewed as The Boss in the streets of Baltimore, but Julio was a Don on a whole other level. He had power and influence to a degree that JR never saw before, not even being around Polo. His reach was international. If he was in Bogota, he had the means to reach out and get you touched here in the U.S., with just a simple phone call, if he wanted to do so. When a boss of Julio's stature called a meeting, you dropped everything and got there expeditiously, because if you didn't, the ramifications and repercussions could be fatal.

Without a second thought, JR shot out to BWI Thurgood Marshall Airport to catch the next flight to New York. He took Demon along with him, just in case anything jumped off. The flight to New York was only an hour long. When they reached LaGuardia Airport, they made a beeline for the transportation section of the airport to hail down a cab. Once inside the cab, they instructed the cab driver to take them to the Ritz-Carlton on 57th Street in midtown Manhattan. As the cab driver weaved his way through the hectic New York City traffic en route to the hotel, JR and Demon tried to figure out what prompted this meeting to be called. They both were nervous.

"Yo, what do you think Julio wants? It can't be because I owe him money that's for damn sure," JR reasoned.

He was right. In all of the years that he dealt with Julio, he always got him his money on time, without ever being short. Besides, if you were to come up short with his money, you wouldn't receive a phone call for a meeting. Chances are, you would wake up in the middle of the night with the barrel of a gun stuck in your mouth, the safety off, and death imminent.

"Boss, I have not a clue. Maybe somebody is trying to move in on our action in Bmore and he needs us to take care of that problem. I'm just grabbing at straws for real. Shit, it could be anything. We will just have to wait and see. Either way, I ride or die with you. I got your back," Demon spoke directly. He was a loyal soldier, down for the cause.

"I never doubted that for a second, fam. I feel the same way, cause you my nigga," JR chimed in.

JR trusted Demon with his life. He was the one person in his crew that he would bet the house on remaining loyal, no matter what the situation was. If he got knocked, he wouldn't break because he was that solid of a soldier. He was built to be on the frontline, always ready to go to war. He didn't care if it was somebody with power on the level of Julio, or just a rogue street cat that had issues with JR. Anybody could get it if they crossed The Boss. That was just how he got down. JR gave him a new life when he gave him a job, and he was eternally grateful. Before he became his head of security, his life had no focus as he just bounced from job to job. Now he had one clear mission, and that was to ensure the safety of JR. He was down to catch a bullet for him if need be.

For the rest of the cab ride, the two changed the subject, in an attempt to ease the nervousness they both felt about this last minute meeting. They were so caught up in conversation that they didn't realize they had reached the hotel until the driver got their attention.

"That will be twenty-five dollars, gentleman," the cab driver said with a thick Middle Eastern accent.

"Here you go, fella. Keep the change," JR responded.

He gave the cab driver a hundred bill as he and Demon hopped out of the cab. Getting a seventy-five dollar tip was good come up for him, no doubt. It was now time to for them to go inside and see what the business was with Julio. No matter how things played out, they planned to conduct themselves like nothing but true G's. Anything less would be ungodly.

5

JR and Demon entered the upscale hotel en route to the meeting. As they walked through the lobby towards the elevator, they were greeted by strange looks and stares from the many well to do Caucasian guests. JR just laughed them off, because if these uppity white folks only knew that the little black kid that they were turning their nose up to was rich enough to buy them all ten times over, they would probably shit on themselves. When they reached the elevator, they entered and JR pushed the button for the penthouse suite as Julio had instructed.

They got off the elevator on the correct floor and walked towards the room. JR noticed the two buff Colombian henchmen stationed outside of Julio's suite. He knew that they were strapped with some serious artillery. He and Demon didn't bother to bring any weapons because it would've been pointless. They wouldn't be allowed to bring them into the meeting after they were patted down anyway. Plus, if Julio wanted to kill him, it was little that he and Demon would be able to do to defend against his well-trained army of assassins.

"JR, my main man, how's it going? I see you brought your pit bull along with you. What's up, Demon?" Rafael, one of the security men, uttered.

Demon nodded his head in response as a sign of respect. Rafael was the head of Julio's security detail, and had developed a cordial relationship with JR over the years of his dealings with Julio. Rafael and Demon had a mutual respect for each other's passion for administering bodily harm. The two security guards patted them down and saw that they weren't packing any heat.

"Business is good, as usual, my Colombian brother. When the boss calls, I'm here as his humble servant," JR replied.

Rafael smiled as he opened the door to let them in. It was game time.

Once inside the luxurious suite, JR set his eyes on Julio, who was seated along with three other stone-faced Colombian cats on the ritzy furniture in the living room section of the suite. JR had never laid eyes on these cats before, and the looks on their faces suggested that they were all about business. He looked at Demon and they both nodded as if to confirm that their being nervous had now escalated to being scared as hell that death, for some unknown reason, lay ahead for them both.

The other three men could sense their fear. The tension in the room was eased when Julio sprung up from the couch and greeted JR and Demon with a huge grin on his face. The other three men broke their stone-faced looks as well and replaced them with high spirited laughter. JR's heart dropped to the floor. He felt relieved.

"JR, my Nubian brother, I'm glad you could make it for the meeting. You look like you saw a ghost or something. What, did you think I called you here to whack you or something?" Julio asked. He formed his fingers into the shape of a gun, pointed it at JR, and simulated firing a shot. JR played along and acted as though he'd been shot, and fell to the ground. He got up off the floor and tried to laugh off the fact that he was sure that death had called his number a few seconds ago.

"Honestly, I didn't know what to think, Julio," JR replied.

"No worries, my friend, no worries. You're with family here. Come meet my brothers. Come. You too, Demon, come on. What kind of name is Demon, anyway? I should call you Satan instead, huh?" Julio joked as he playfully punched Demon in his massive bicep.

Demon cracked a half smile and nodded. They all walked over to the area where the other men were seated.

"Julio, is this the one you call the money machine because he makes us so much dinero?" One of the men asked. He was short with a portly shape, but bore a striking resemblance to Julio.

"Yup, this is the one and only, JR. He's my main man. He takes the coca I give him and makes it disappear like magic in no time," Julio joked.

"Well, that's what I do. That's why they call me the Snow Man," JR chimed in.

"JR, these are my brothers, Javier, Armando, and Hector. I have told them so many good things about you and they flew all the way here from Colombia to meet you in person," Julio stated. His laughter was now replaced with a more serious tone. JR shook hands with the three men. Demon sat in the background as a silent observer.

"It's an honor to meet you all. So, what's the purpose of this meeting that I had to come here so suddenly?" JR asked.

"Ahhh, yessss, of course, I was getting around to that. I brought you here to talk about a new business opportunity. I wanna talk about expansion," Julio replied eagerly.

"I'm all ears, Julio. If you're talking mucho dinero, I'm all ears. Spit game to me," JR said confidently. He was now totally relaxed and eager to hear Julio's plan.

"I knew you would be, and that's why you're here. Tell me something, what do you know about this new drug they call Molly that has all the young people going crazy?" Julio inquired.

"That's mostly for White kids in the Midwest and out in California or some shit. I saw on the news a few times how some crazy hillbillies was making that shit in a trailer and blew themselves up. I know a few cats in Bmore that sell them in the clubs here and a lot of the young kids in the city are starting to use them. That's never been my thing. I'm an old school dope boy," JR replied honestly.

"Ahhh, times are changing, my friend. Times are truly changing. Mollys are the wave of the future and I plan to corner the market. It's relatively inexpensive to make, and the profit margin is more than triple what I'm making now, selling cocaine," Julio stated as he puffed on a fat Cuban cigar.

"Did you say triple the profit? I know I didn't just hear you say that, did I?" JR asked. His eyes were wide open and full of enthusiasm. His mind raced with figures as he calculated how much more cash he could make if what Julio had just spoken was true.

"I see that caught your interest, huh?" Armando asked with a big grin on his face. Standing almost six feet tall, Armando was the tallest and most handsome of the brothers.

"Hell, yeah! Money talks in my world!" JR declared.

"I thought you would see things my way. JR, you're a go getta and that's why I like you so much. You know some of my Colombians compadres don't really care for African Americans because they see them as lazy. Me, on the other hand, I have a broader perspective on these types of things. I had to convince them that you were nothing like that at all. I told them, 'my man JR, he's different.' You're a smart man and you recognize how to seize the moment when opportunity presents itself. Am I right?" Julio asked.

"Absolutely right," JR answered. He brushed off the racist tone of Julio's statement. He couldn't care less about being seen as inferior or trying to promote racial harmony. He was focused on the money. His favorite color wasn't black or white—he was all about the green.

"That's what I wanted to hear. Now this is what I'm proposing. I wanna set you up in business as my main distributor of Mollys, not just in Baltimore, but the entire East Coast. I want you to look at this new business venture as a promotion. JR, my friend, you are about to move up in the world," Julio replied.

"That sounds good, but I don't know anything about making that shit. What about the law? Don't they hand out more time for manufacturing those synthetic drugs?" JR asked.

Julio's brothers looked at him with concern. He shot them back a look of confidence to assure them that he would handle easing JR's concerns.

"Relax, my young amigo, relax. You have no worries. We already have that covered. You see, we have already been dabbling in the market out West, and pretty much have that area locked down. We have manufacturing plants set up in clandestine locations across the country to make the shit ourselves. We're not relying on no ass backwards white farm boys to make it for us. We have hired some of the best chemists in the world to make the shit right. Our product won't be watered down or cut. It's gonna be that real deal shit. It's gonna have all these young kids going crazy, trying to spend their parents' life savings trying to buy it. As for the law, that's not a problem either. You have the full protection and support of my organization. All of our resources will be at your disposal.

"I already have several cities picked out that we can set up shop in and flood the streets with our product. All you have to do is put your people in place to make it happen. I'm counting on you to get the job done. I know you can handle it, my friend. JR, I can assure you that if you follow my directions and do exactly what I tell you to do, you will have no problems. You have to keep a low profile and not draw unnecessary attention to yourself. Make sure that the violence and beefing is kept to a minimum, because senseless killing is an easy way to get ya self on the radar of the law as a top priority to come after. Finally, my friend, make sure that you have the most loyal soldiers around you, because one fucking rat in the bunch can fuck up the whole game," Julio stated confidently.

Julio had the serious look of a mafia Don on his face. His brothers appeared just as stern and assured that this plan would work. JR was in the company of made men. The kind of men that the FBI or DEA never got anywhere near when they made arrests. They had international political ties that could get them political asylum if needed to avoid incarceration. According to Julio, JR would be afforded similar insulation from prosecution. He had to decide whether or not he was ready to swim with the big dogs. Once he made a commitment with cats like Julio and his brothers, there was no turning back. When you get inducted into a crime organization of this stature, your commitment was for life or death. He looked at Demon, who had observed everything.

Demon gave him the nod of approval. No more needed to be said.

"I'm down. Let's get paid," JR stated bluntly. It was a no brainer for him. He had just gone from being a hood celebrity, to a member of an international crime syndicate. His balls just grew ten times bigger. He already felt untouchable on the streets of Baltimore. Now he felt like he could walk on water without getting wet.

"Now that's what I'm talking about. We can talk later about the specifics of everything. Now we must celebrate. Ladies, it's time to party!" Julio stated excitedly. He clapped his hands, and just like magic, ten of the finest pieces of Colombian ass came forth from behind the closed doors of the master bedroom suite.

"Julio, you dirty dog, you!" JR joked. Two of the beautiful women came and sat on his lap. He could feel a bulge developing in his crotch.

"What can I say? I love fine pussy as much as I love money. Demon, get your evil ass over here and get in on this. Enjoy, my friends! Enjoy!" Julio demanded.

Julio turned on the stereo with the remote control and in no time, sultry native Colombian music played in the background. He began to grind on one of the beautiful women and plant kisses all over her neck. The two women that sat on JR's lap led him back into one of the other bedrooms. Demon followed suit with another one of the young ladies. All of the Gomez brothers selected the women of their choice to ravish for the night. The bar was stocked with enough liquor for all to drink until they passed out. This was a festive occasion. They all planned to enjoy the moment while it lasted. Tomorrow, the reality of JR's new life would begin.

6

Six months had passed since JR's sit down meeting with Julio and his brothers in New York City, and everything went down as planned. Julio was true to his word in opening up the floodgates to a sea of new money to JR and he was happy to receive it all. With his help, JR was able to setup manufacturing plants in Philadelphia, Atlanta, Charlotte, Miami, and Boston to produce as much product as was needed to feed the public demand. The plants were staffed by well-trained chemists from all over the world that were handpicked by the Gomez brothers to concoct the new "It" drug in abundance.

Initially, JR sent Demon and Diggy on road trips along with a few hardheaded goons for backup to oversee the local drug runners that he hired in each city. Over time, he developed a relationship with a few local hustlers who showed leadership potential, in every city, and he let them do their own thing. As long as they came back with his money as expected when he sent Demon or Diggy to collect, there would be no problems. With the support of Julio's organization and the legwork put in by the Money Kings crew, the word had spread up and down the East Coast that JR was the man to see about the purchase of Mollys if you wanted them wholesale. He had the whole market in a vice grip.

JR's stranglehold on the Molly drug trade in

Baltimore was even tighter. A week after he had everything setup for his distribution network, JR literally cornered the market on all sales of Mollys across the State of Maryland. He expanded the reach of his drug empire to include upscale communities in the county regions where all of the rich white college kids loved to party and pop Mollys all night long. The few cats that were in the business before he got involved were given a choice. They either got down with JR's team or faced getting laid down by Demon and his goons. Most of them were wise and decided to join forces with JR. As for the few that tried to play hardball, well let's just say their life span was cut very short. Those county white boys wanted no parts of a war with some wild thugs from the city streets of Baltimore. JR now had young White drug dealers selling his pills on college campuses across the state. He was the MAN.

JR was not only successful in setting up shop in the county areas of the state, but he also created a new lane in the city for his product. He had his crew give out free testers at the Money Kings Bar and Lounge and all of the other top party spots in the city to partygoers that were known to indulge in drug use. They were a part of a free spirited crowd that was uninhibited and open to trying a new drug. Once they got a taste of his product, they flocked to it like flies to shit. The money he made from selling Mollys dwarfed the money he had made traditionally selling cocaine and heroin because it was so cheap to make. He made more money in the last three months than he had made in his two best years of selling coke and dope out in the streets. If he had known about the money making potential of this wonder drug years ago, he would be a billionaire by now.

In a mood to celebrate, JR sat in the backseat of

his Rolls Royce Phantom as his driver, Allen, pulled up to the Money Kings Lounge. Allen was a new youngster on the team. He was only twenty years old and wet behind the ears. He wanted to hustle because he needed money to pay for college, but JR could tell when he first met him that he wasn't cut out for the street life. He was too soft, and still had a conscience. With those two traits, a brother wouldn't last long in a cutthroat world. So instead of hitting him off with a pack to work a corner for him, JR gave him a job as his personal driver whenever he needed to be chauffeured around. He paid him two grand a week, even if he didn't need his services for that particular week. That was enough money for him to be able to pay for college, get his own place, and be able to take care of his sickly mother. JR knew he was a good kid and considered helping him as a way to do a good deed in light of all of his other wicked deeds.

JR and his crew sat outside for a minute to observe the scene and admire the fruits of his labor. The Money Kings Lounge was his brainchild. He wanted to create a party experience in the city where everybody could party and have a good time in the most luxurious venue possible. He succeeded in doing so when the club had its grand opening four years ago. The lounge had four levels with each one catering to a different musical style from hip-hop, r and b, house music to reggae. Each level had a huge dance floor and open bar area. There were scantily clad females dancing on top of strategically placed mini-stage areas throughout the club. Anything that one could imagine that they wanted in a nightclub was made available at the lounge.

The place had a capacity of three thousand people, but he was sure that there had to be several more hundred people inside. He was in violation of the city occupancy code, but he didn't care. The worst thing that would happen if the fire marshal came and cited him was that he would get a fine. He would pay that fine happily, in exchange for raking in all the dough he made at club legally and illegally. The lounge was always jam packed inside, and the line was always around the corner with anxious partygoers waiting for a chance to get in. JR had the hottest spot in the city, hands down, and he was damn proud.

"Yo, I'm trying to leave here with something new on my arm tonight," G Money bragged as he sipped a glass of champagne.

"Man, you know your ass ain't pushing up on nothin' new tonight. You're scared of new pussy. Plus, you know your girl would kick your ass if she found out you was out here messing around. Elaine looks like the type to smell a nigga balls when he come home to see if he's been fucking another bitch," Demon joked. He sat up front with Allen. G-Money and Diggy rode in the back with JR.

"You ain't got no game, fool. You couldn't get Superhead to give you some head, even if you paid her five stacks," Diggy chimed in on the shit on G Money parade.

"Man, y'all can say whatever you want, but you know damn well I get more hoes than the both of you lames," G Money shot back.

He tried to protect his rep, but the truth was the truth. He had no game when it came to the ladies. He was shy and bashful. He wouldn't approach a bad chick in the club unless he was drunk. The liquid courage put the battery in his back and gave him the heart to push up on a female. Without it, he would just stutter and embarrass himself in front of just about any good-looking chick he approached. It was obvious that he was irritated by Demon and Diggy riding him so hard.

"Aight y'all, let my man be. G-Money, you're the man, homey. They're just jealous. Demon knows he can't get no pussy because his dick is so small from lifting all those weights, and Diggy ain't getting no play because his breath smells like a baboon's ass. Don't pay those fools no mind. Go ahead and get yours tonight! You're a boss. Like TI said, *you can have whatever you liiikkkke, yeahhhh*!" JR sang offbeat with the music.

G Money felt ten feet tall because it appeared that JR had his back. His cosign was all he needed to feel confident enough to put his best mack game down tonight. In reality, JR was just gassing him up to make a fool of himself so he could get a good laugh at his expense as well.

"I ain't got time to be sittin' out here with you fools. I'm fixin' to go up in this club tonight, get my drink on, and poke something. Y'all coming with me or what?" G Money asked. He sipped the last of the bottle of champagne he had been nursing the entire ride to the lounge.

"Let's get it!" JR said bluntly.

When JR opened the car door, you would've thought it was Jay Z or Denzel stepping out of the car. The thirsty females in the line damn near creamed on themselves as he walked towards the front door. His aura of power had them all mesmerized. Everybody in the city knew who he was. All of them clamored for a chance to ride on his love stick once, just for bragging rights and the faint hope that he might choose one of them to be his side bitch. The whole city knew that Rochelle was his wifey, so being his off and on jump off was the best spot they could hope to claim.

JR gave the security guards a pound as he entered the club with his crew close behind him. He shook hands with several people throughout the club that were eager to get his attention. They all acted as though they were personal friends of JR, but in all reality, they were nothing more than nameless faces in the crowd. They were paying customers that increased his bankroll. A few fake smiles and handshakes were well worth his time if it meant more cash flow into his already bloated bank accounts.

Tonight was a special night because JR's young rap artist, Hostile, was scheduled to perform his new single, "Countin' Stacks", along with a slew of other songs from his new mixtape called, *These Bmore Streets Raised Me*. The mixtape was straight dope, raw and uncut. Thanks to JR's power and influence, he was able to get his songs in heavy rotation at all of the local radio stations. He sold thousands of copies of his CD on the streets out of the trunk of his car. JR made sure that his pockets stayed swollen and that he had the best of everything.

Hostile, whose real name was Titus Clark, stood just a hair above five feet four inches tall and had a stocky, muscular physique. What he lacked in height, he made up for in talent because this kid could spit rhymes with the best lyricists in the game. He held his own in ciphers across the country with some of the hottest freestylers in the streets. He wasn't a gangster by any means. His rhymes were about partying, getting white boy wasted, and sexing the finest females. He was a finesse rapper with a smooth flow like TI. He wore a truckload of platinum jewelry around his neck and on his wrist. He drove around town in a deep grey BMW 745i custom fitted with twenty-inch chrome wheels. His swag was on full display at all times. He made the other aspiring rap artists in the city jealous, but he didn't care. With JR's backing, none of them fools was bold enough to step to him with any drama.

As Hostile was about to take the stage, JR directed Trixie, the bartender, to send up ten bottles of Moet to the VIP lounge where he and his crew were headed. She complied with his demands and had a waiter bring them to the area in record time. The rest of his top soldiers were already in the VIP section holding court with a slew of Baltimore's finest sack chasers. They all exchanged pounds and hugs. They had a clear view of the main stage area where Hostile was busy hyping up the crowd. The ladies went crazy when he ripped off his wife beater in the middle of one of his songs. His firm pectoral muscles and diamond cut abs made their mouths water. All of the thugs in the crowd bopped their heads to the beat as he performed song after song. They couldn't front on his talent because the boy had skills. He performed a 30-minute set that had the crowd in an uproar.

"JR, you gotta get ya boy a record deal with somebody. That boy can get it in. He's nice with it. I fucks with him heavy," Diggy shouted over the music.

"I'm working on it, fam, but these record labels don't wanna show a Baltimore artist no love in the business. Plus, when I approach them about him, they get scared off by me and see me as just another nigga on some thug shit and not about his business. I'm getting to the point where I might just have to fuck around and put my own money behind him for him to get on," JR replied. He was strongly considering this option.

"That's not a bad idea, boss. The streets respect you, so you know all these lil' thug cats will buy his shit. I'm tired of seeing rappers from other cities gettin' on, but nobody from here representing how we live," G Money cut in.

"I hear you, homey. We'll see what happens. Right

now, I wanna propose a toast. I need for everybody to get quiet for a minute," JR demanded loudly.

All conversation ceased. JR had the floor to speak his mind. He had finished off a bottle and a half of champagne by himself, and was definitely feeling the effects.

"What's up, big dawg? What's on ya mind?" Demon asked as he sipped on a Hurricane mixed drink.

"I wanted to take the time out to thank all my niggas for all the hard work y'all puttin' in out in dem streets. Profits are up to an unbelievable level, unlike ever before. I didn't build this empire by myself. I couldn't have done it without every single one of you. We're a team. Hell, we're a family. Even when somebody got knocked off, I'm proud to know that none of my soldiers turned rat. We're just not built like all these other bitch ass niggas out here. We eat, sleep, and drink this thug life shit. Floyd Mayweather has The Money Team and I can respect that because he runs the boxing game and he's a boss at what he does. However, when it comes to the streets, we're the crew of all crews and that's why we're called the Money Kings. We're all bosses in our own right, but I'm the head boss of this thing of ours.

"I wanna start a clothing line with our name on it. I'ma have everybody rockin' our shit. I can see it now. We're gonna let the world know who we be. By the time we're done, the streets will be singing our praises as the best to ever do it, excluding nobody. To show my appreciation for all of your hard work, I got a surprise lined up. I set it up with my man, Levi, at the Mercedes dealer in Laurel for every one of my top lieutenants to get a brand new 2014 Mercedes s550 with the Money Kings license tag on the front. The whips are already paid for, and all you gotta do is go pick out what color you want. Since we're a boss crew, it's only right that we ride like bosses accordingly. From here on out, we're fixin' to get turnt up to a whole other level. Does anybody object?" JR asked. The room was silent.

"Hell naw, none of you fools better not object or I'ma stomp a mud hole in ya ass," Demon threatened jokingly. Everybody else laughed as well as they continued to sip champagne.

"To the Money Kings! We run this shit here!" Diggy chimed in.

Everybody raised their glasses in a toast and took the champagne straight to the head. Not only did JR buy new whips for his closest associates, Diggy, Demon, and G Money, but he also bought them for Banks, Joel, Nitty, and Sherman who were also top ranking lieutenants in the crime family. Truth be told, they were all in a state of shock. Nobody could believe that JR had just dropped almost a million dollars in total to buy whips for his top-level workers like it was nothing. However, business had truly been good to them over the past year. He figured the best way to show appreciation was to reward his team by sharing the wealth. He had already given them all a bump in their weekly pay, but this level of generosity was over the top. They partied the rest of the night away and reveled in the moment. The Money Kings were on top of the drug world, whether the haters liked it or not, and JR sat at the helm all alone. He couldn't have scripted this whole scenario any better if he tried. Living the good life was all he had on his mind. Anything else just didn't matter, point blank.

In the midst of the commotion and celebration, Hostile and his entourage had entered the VIP section of the club to join the party. He gave daps to all the crew and made his way over to where JR was seated.

JR embraced him like he would a little brother who he hadn't seen in awhile. Hostile took a seat next to him. He sat back and observed all of the fine pieces of ass that were littered throughout the section.

"What up, lil' homey? I see you did ya thing tonight. You had the crowd amped up, fam. You think you're ready for that prime time spotlight?" JR asked enthusiastically.

"Hell yeah, I'm ready. JR, you know none of these fools can see me on this microphone," Hostile shot back. He was cocky and confident in his flow, but he had a right to be. He had the goods to be one of the best to ever to do it, for sure. All he needed was a shot.

"Well, we're gonna make this happen real soon," JR promised.

"U know me, fam. You're da boss and I'm riding with you. Whatever you say, goes," he uttered in response.

"Well, I say you need to get up on one of these fine honeys up in here. Hey Renee, come here girl. I need you to take care of my man here. Show him how the Money Kings get down," JR yelled across the room to a sexy looking light brown-skinned cutie with an ass that was as beautiful as her face.

She walked across the room and sat down on Hostile's lap. She was his for the night. Being connected to the most respected drug crew in the city certainly had its benefits, and Hostile enjoyed every one of them.

7

JR dipped out of the party a little earlier than he had originally planned. He knew that he could trust Demon and Diggy to close up shop at the club in his absence. He had to make another stop before he headed home. He was pissy drunk from downing so much champagne, and he had smoked several blunts throughout the course of the day. He was super horny and in need of some female company. JR got Allen to take him by one of his regular side chick's condominium in downtown Baltimore. Her name was Roshonda Monet. She was a stunningly beautiful dark skinned sista from East Africa. She spoke several different African dialects, as well as French and Japanese. She had been in America for over ten years, so her accent had all but faded away.

When JR saw her thunderous chocolate-coated thighs and equally appealing video model like derriere walk by him at the Money Kings Lounge one night almost a year ago, he made it his mission to get to know her. The next time she came to the club, he spotted her in the crowd as she partied with her girls, and got her attention. As they conversed, he ran his game down on her so smoothly that she was hooked instantly by his charm. Not too soon afterwards, they developed the perfect homey lover friend relationship that fit just right for both them.

Roshonda didn't care that JR was married,

because she wasn't looking for a serious relationship. Her career as a translator for the United Nations kept her extremely busy and constantly on the road. She just needed a man to satisfy her sexually and to keep her company when the urge hit her. She wanted no strings attached because it kept her life simple. She had no children and planned to keep it that way. Her arrangement with JR worked out just fine for both of them. He got what he wanted and she got what she needed. Everything was all good.

JR had called Roshonda before he left the club to let her know that he was on his way over to her place. It was almost two in the morning, so she knew this was nothing but a booty call. She didn't care, because she was in the mood for a good sexin' anyway. She had been stressed at work recently and needed to release it all. Some good sweat drenched, hard-core, thumpin' sex was the best remedy to cure her ailment. JR was the man for the job because he never left her disappointed.

When they arrived at her place, JR instructed Allen to wait for him in the parking lot. He staggered out of the car because his vertigo was off keel, but he managed to pull himself together somewhat by the time he reached the front door of the building. He rang her apartment buzzer number in the main lobby and Roshonda buzzed him into the building. He got on the elevator and got off on the fourth floor. When he reached her condo, he turned the door knob and entered. She always left the door unlocked for him when she knew he was on his way over.

"Hey, baby, come on in. I'm in the bedroom," Roshonda yelled loudly.

JR walked thru the condo en route to her bedroom. All the lights were out and he bumped into the sofa and an end table along the way to meet her.

When he entered the room, the only light that he saw was the dim reflection of the moon that pierced thru the window blinds. Even though it was dark, Roshonda had one of those asses you could spot anywhere. It was heart shaped and so phat that it took both hands to manage. Her tiny little waist made it stick out that much more. That ass couldn't come from anywhere else but mother Africa, the birthplace of civilization. She knew it was a gift from her ancestors and had used it to her advantage all of her life to drive men crazy. She was a nasty girl who always kept the upper hand with men because her sex game was top notch. She knew she was working with something potent and made sure that no man ever forgot that fact. JR was no different. Her pussy had him hooked and he couldn't leave it alone even if he wanted to try to do so.

Roshonda was stretched out on the bed with nothing on but her birthday suit. She laid on her stomach with that Godsend of an ass of hers in plain view for JR to see. His dick got hard from the thought of what he was about to do with that plump rump. She lit up a candle on her nightstand to give him a better view of all of her sexiness. She was covered in a mango scented body oil that made her smooth dark skin glisten so elegantly. JR sat down on the edge of the bed to regain his composure because his head was buzzing.

On the ride to her house, to top off all the liquor he drank at the club and the weed he smoked earlier, he had also popped a Molly for the first time. Diggy had tried it a few times and told him how good the sex was when he took them and it made him curious. It wasn't coke or dope, so he figured that there was no way he could get hooked on them. If it made sex that much better, he was down to give them a shot. He let his curiosity get the best of him and he was about to find out for himself if what Diggy said was the truth.

"What's up, sexy? Mama's kitty cat has been missing her bad boy. You can't keep that python inside your pants away from me for too long, because she gets lonely without him," Roshonda uttered.

She took her hand and smacked her ass. It jiggled with a rhythm so fluid that JR was clearly turned on. She laid back comfortably on her extra fluffy down feather pillows and grabbed her chilled glass of red Sangria off the nightstand. She cocked her legs wide open so that JR could get a good view of her recently bikini line waxed vajayjay. To be so thick, she was mad flexible. JR found this out for himself after he bent her legs back over her head several times while he pounded her sweet tender coochie like a construction worker working a jackhammer.

"Damn, woman, you sure do know how to greet a brother," JR stated as his eyes were fixated on her pelvic region.

"I don't believe in wasting time. If you see something that you like, feel free to dive on in and help yourself. Come feast on all this women here," Roshonda suggested strongly. A dude would have to be gay if he didn't wanna tap that ass at least once. Hell, even if he was gay, she was so fine that she could make a gay dude think twice about making a change in his sexuality.

"Shit, you ain't said nothing but a word. I'm on it," JR said excitedly. He licked his lips eagerly because he knew he was about to tear some shit up. He was about to go into beast mode on that ass.

Roshonda ran her hands along the outsides of her breasts. They were equally as appealing as her backside. They were a size 36C and when she shook them in her hands, JR envisioned making them both melt inside his mouth like two chocolate covered M and M's. She fondled her nipples to make them get rock solid. JR pulled his shirt over his head and threw it on the floor. He stood up and undid his pants. He let them drop to the floor along with his boxer shorts. He stood before her with his dick hard as granite and ready to bang her pussy walls until they caved in. He crawled up on the bed and got on top of her. When his lips met hers, he felt a strange sensation like he had never felt before. His entire body was on fire. He felt a tingly sensation all over when his naked body collided with hers. Words couldn't describe the intense rush he experienced. The Molly pill had taken effect.

"Damn, mommy, your body feels so fucking good right now. I wanna eat ya ass alive!" JR declared.

He caressed her body and kissed her from head to toe. He got down on his knees and between her thighs to taste her sweet spot. His licked her pussy from left to right and up and down, so passionately that she came all over his face in under five minutes. After her second orgasm, she tried to push his head away, because she had lost all control of her bodily functions, but JR was locked into her pussy so tight that he refused to stop. He was determined to get one more blast of cum out of her before he let her have her pussy back. For now, it was under his tongue's control and forced to do as it commanded.

"JR, that feels too fucking good. Please stop! I can't take it! Ohhh shit. I'm about to cum! You ain't never eat my goodies like this before. You got me about to lose my mind up in here. What the hell are you doing to me?" she asked as he inserted three fingers inside of her.

"I'm giving you what your body needs. Now shut up and enjoy it!" he said bossily. His fingers were drenched with her juices. Her insides were slippery wet. She spread her legs wider so that he could insert another finger inside of her to help the other three in their quest to make her cum again.

"Yes, daddy, don't stop! Oh, how I missed this, you nasty son of a bitch, you. JR you ain't no joke. Give it to me, baby!" she begged.

The walls of her vagina contracted around his fingers. The sensation she experienced forced her eyes to shut and made her mind go blank. JR had total control of her physical being. While he fucked her pussy with his fingers, his tongue did a nasty number on her perky nipples. Her entire body convulsed and shook violently. She wanted to cry, because his sex felt so damn good. JR was just getting started. He had much more in store for her.

"Tell me what you want me to do to you, bitch?" he asked in an aggressive voice. He sped up the pace of the thrusts of his fingers.

"I want you to take that big dick of yours and stick it in my mouth. Give me every inch of it, until no more can fit. I wanna suck it until you cum and then drink every drop of that sweet cum of yours," she replied. As professional as she was at work, in the bedroom she was a low down dirty freak, open to the kinkiest shit. JR was only happy to oblige her inner slut. It was the least he could do.

"After I cum in your mouth, then what you want me to do?" JR further quizzed.

"I want you to bend me over this bed and fuck the dog shit outta me with that manly dick of yours. Feed it to my pussy until it can't cum anymore. I want you to spank my ass while you're fucking me. Come get this pussy now!" she yelled.

JR wasted no time in flipping her over and giving her what she desired. He lifted her ass in the air and just looked at it for a minute to admire its majesty.

For special effects, she wiggled it in his face a few times. He took his hand and smacked it twice. The stinging feeling hurt, but she screamed for more pain. She liked it rough and raunchy. JR took his dick and shoved it inside of her forcefully. She loved the rough feeling and relaxed her body to enjoy getting fucked by a real man who knew how to handle all of her thickness. He made her come once again. A smile came across her face while tears poured from her eyes.

Roshonda thanked him for his service to her pussy by taking his penis in her mouth and sucking it until he came all over her face. That was the best nut JR ever had in his life. Rochelle's head game was on point, but Roshonda's was porn star worthy. His entire body felt numb as she kept sucking him until he went limp. He didn't know if it was because her sex was that good, or due to the pill, that he felt like he was having an out of body experience. He could've sworn he was floating in the air looking down on himself having sex with her. He didn't care if it was all real or not. He just knew it felt good. He collapsed on the bed and fell asleep from exhaustion.

When JR woke up, the sun shined bright in his face. He covered his eyes to block it out. Roshonda was on top of him, riding his member like she owned it. The bed rocked back and forth as it swayed with the movement of her hips. JR grabbed a hold of her waist to keep up. He was so out of it after the last go round, that he didn't even feel her suck him off to get him hard again while he slept. It didn't matter. He just laid back and enjoyed the view of her booty in the dresser mirror in front of him as it jiggled.

His mind drifted away for a second because he realized that he had stayed out all night again, and Rochelle would surely be in super bitch mode when he got home. *Fuck it! I'll deal with that later!* He surmised. He had to give this righteous piece of ass on top of him his undivided attention. It was the least he could do. If poppin' Mollys made the sex this good, he and Molly would be getting to know each other a lot better.

8

It was 10 am when Nigel awoke to the sound of his alarm clock going off. It felt good to be able to sleep late for a change. Being your own boss afforded him such a luxury every now and then. To have Nicole as a business partner made him feel comfortable that things would run smoothly in the office without him being there. She went into the office earlier in the morning to open up for business. Every now and then, Nigel needed a break from the fast pace of the real estate world, just to clear his head. Even though he was off from work, he still had a busy day scheduled, filled with a host of things to do.

He reached onto his nightstand to retrieve the remote control to turn on the 47 inch Samsung SMART HDTV. He fumbled with the remote for a few minutes before he finally figured out where the Power button was located. It was Nicole's idea to buy this hi-tech TV that was equipped with Wi-Fi and internet access. He was old school, and didn't see the need to use your TV to get on the internet. That was what he thought his Samsung tablet or desktop computer was made to do. He did, however, love the crystal clear picture that it delivered whenever he took out the time to watch a movie or to catch up on the news.

Once the TV was on, he flipped the channel to CNN to catch up on some of the current events in the news. They happened to be running a segment on the current housing market and how it may be on an incline after several years of market failure. That was good news to Nigel. Despite the last few years being a rough time for the real estate industry as a whole, with so many properties losing substantial market value and multitudes of people losing their homes to foreclosure, Nigel still managed to turn a hefty profit with his business. That was because he bought low cost properties far below their value and sold them at prices affordable enough for the customer.

In the same breath, the prices were still sufficient for him to make a lofty profit in return. He had the benefit of living in a city such as Baltimore, where abandoned homes that were primed for rehabilitation were in abundance for purchase by the wise investor with vision. Nigel utilized the ingenuity and savvy hustling skills that he honed throughout his addiction to take advantage of the opportunities that lay in his path. As a result, he was now the head of a multi-million dollar real estate firm. One of the city's worst menaces was now one of its most respected businessmen. He defined the meaning of a true success story while in recovery.

When he was done watching the news, Nigel jumped in the shower to wash off the sweet smell of the raspberry scented lotion that happened to rub off on him after his intense love making session with Nicole. After he dried off, he used his trimmers to freshen up his salt and pepper beard. He covered his body in cocoa butter to moisturize his skin and sprayed a dash of Perry Ellis Midnight cologne on both sides of his neck. He went into his closet and retrieved a pair of taupe colored khakis and a crisply ironed orange Polo shirt to wear. When he was fully dressed, he gave himself a final glance over in the mirror. Satisfied that he looked suave and debonair, he made his way downstairs to the first floor of his magnificent home.

Nigel had purchased the four thousand square foot palace as a foreclosed property for a fraction of its actual value. It contained four bedrooms and three bathrooms. The kitchen area was huge, with an elegant island area in the center for Nicole to utilize when she prepared dinner for the family. All of the appliances were chrome colored. The family room and living areas were elegantly decorated with trendy furniture and artwork that were all selected by Nicole. She had exquisite taste, so everything was top notch. He built a game room in the basement, so that Malachi and his grandkids could play their video games. He also had his own theater room installed down there for when he wanted to watch a movie on his 100-inch big screen projector, because he rarely had time to go to the movies.

In the backyard, there was an Olympic sized swimming pool that got heavy use during the summer time. Nigel never envisioned himself living in such a place, and yet here he stood. He was now a wealthy man in both spirit and finances. Just like JR, he was a boss in his own right, a master of his own fate. The only difference was that his business was legal.

After grabbing a bagel to eat and drinking his usual cup of coffee, Nigel grabbed the keys to his money green Mercedes E550 and headed towards the garage door. He planned to make a pit stop sometime during the day at Exquisite Custom Detailing to get the ride cleaned up. Once inside, he turned on the XM radio to the Watercolors station to listen to the calming sounds of some smooth jazz. He opened the door of the garage with the remote door opener and pulled his fine European machine out into the driveway to start his journey.

Unlike JR, Nigel didn't need a lot full of fancy cars to display his wealth. His E class Benz was enough for him to get around town and do his business in style. He didn't want any unwarranted attention being thrown his way by the cops because he was a black man driving in several different expensive luxury cars. He also saw that having more than one car was an unnecessary waste of money. That extra couple of hundred grand could be put to better use with him buying more properties. He never bought his cars outright, but leased them in the business' name and wrote the monthly payments off as a business expense. He did his best to live a modest suburban life, without drama. He had enough of that from his former life to reflect on, if he needed a reminder. Slow motion and drama free was the perfect mode of life for him nowadays.

Nigel's first stop of the day was at AATC, the treatment center where he began his recovery process after he came home from jail. He had an appointment today with his former counselor, Frank Mackie, and the program director, George Mason. Every now and then, Nigel would check in with Frank to let him know how he was doing with his recovery process. On occasion, he would serve as a guest speaker at one of the program's group sessions. He was grateful for all of the support and counsel that Frank provided him during his early struggles with his disease. Without his guidance, Nigel knew that his getting clean wouldn't have happened.

To show his appreciation, Nigel planned to make a substantial financial donation to the program to help with its efforts to heal the sin sick souls of Baltimore City. He had heard about the recent federal budget cuts, and how they had decreased the availability of funds for treatment services, and figured that he could help to bridge the gap that this created. He reasoned that he had the financial means to assist, and felt that it was his duty as a recovering addict to help the next addict struggling with the same disease.

When he pulled up at the center, he parked his car in front of the facility. As he approached the building, he was overcome with mixed emotions as he watched the helpless addicts out front, still suffering the ill effects of years of drug abuse. He thought about how that used to be him, and felt grateful for how far he had come in life to reach his current state of inner peace. He spoke and walked past them into the facility. He reached the reception area and got the receptionist to call Frank's office. In a matter of minutes, Frank emerged in the lobby to greet him.

"Nigel Hawkins, man look at you. Brother, you done went all big time on me, I see," Frank joked. He was truly proud of Nigel and all that he had accomplished. To see how far he had come in life made his work fulfilling.

"Nah, that's not me, brother. I'm blessed and highly favored is all," Nigel replied humbly.

The two men embraced and Frank led Nigel down the hallway to the Director's office. Frank knocked on the door. Mr. Mason greeted them both with a firm handshake. Once inside, they took a seat at the conference table.

"Mr. Hawkins, on behalf of the program, I just want to say it is an honor to have you as an alumnus. Frank has told me a lot about you and your charitable work in the community. Please know that I can't put it into words what your contribution means to this facility and the things that we will be able to do for the addicts that need help so badly," Mr. Mason stated with deep sincerity.

"It's the least that I can do. This program helped to save my life. You have a fine man here in Frank Mackie. I hope you take good care of him," Nigel replied in a joking tone.

"Of course we do. Frank's my man," Mr. Mason reassured him.

Nigel reached into his briefcase and pulled out his checkbook. He wrote a check in the amount of one hundred grand, payable to the program. Even though the donation was tax deductible, the benefit for Nigel was purely a spiritual one of infinite value. When he handed the check to Mr. Mason, he almost passed out when he saw the amount. To give away one hundred stacks for a good cause was nothing to Nigel. He donated money on a regular basis to several charities throughout the city. He also helped to establish a college fund through the real estate agency that helped at least a handful of underprivileged inner city high school graduates per year pay for college tuition for a full four-year term. He had taken so much from the community in his past that he felt that this was the best way for him to atone for his sins.

"Mr. Hawkins, this is certainly very generous of you. Frank told me that you wanted to make a donation, but wow this is much more than I expected. After I tell the board of directors, they'll probably want to rename this place after you. Dear sweet mother of Jesus!" Mr. Mason shouted. He was elated. His mind raced with visions of the things that he would be able to do with the funds to upgrade the program.

"It's no problem at all. The only request I have is that you continue doing the good work for these clients that need the help. Show me more results and there will be more of that to come your way. Not to cut this short, gentleman, but I have busy day and need to get moving," Nigel stated. He got up out of his seat and exchanged goodbyes with Frank and Mr. Mason before he made his way out of the facility back to his car.

Driving had a calming effect on Nigel. It gave him time alone to think about things clearly, with no distractions. He came up with some of his best ideas in times like this. At night when he couldn't sleep, he would jump in his ride, turn on some old school R and B music, and just cruise down the highway until he felt himself getting tired. He would get lost in his thoughts as his head bopped to the music.

He was at the intersection of Charles Street and 33rd street in east Baltimore when a scraggly looking man darted out in front of his car and caused him to mash down on his brakes. He looked a little closer, and the man looked familiar to him. It was his old running partner, Fats. The jeans that he had on were dingy and filled with holes. He had on what looked like it used to be a white Karl Kani t-shirt. The shirt was so dirty that it appeared to be stained the color of yellow piss. He had on a pair of run down Air Jordan Nikes that were so beat up that Mike himself would be ashamed to have his named associated with the sneakers. Clearly, drugs had gotten the best of him. Judging by the neighborhood he was in, he was more than likely en route to go cop.

Nigel pulled to the side of the road and rolled down his window. "Hey Fats, get ya ass out the street, fool. Come here, man!" Nigel yelled.

Fats turned around in response to the voice and almost fell down in the street. He was so high that he didn't even know it was Nigel at first. Once he gathered himself together, he walked towards the car. As he got closer to the car, he recognized his old friend. They used to run the streets all night together, but today they were on different paths.

"It's my main man, Nigel Hawkins. What's happening, blood? Look at this ride. Man, this is sweet. I see you, son. You are doin' it big, brother, looking all professional. I'm proud of how you've cleaned yourself up. You used to be a rundown junkie like me. Now look at you, owning all of them houses and shit. I know you loaded. Man, why don't you help a brother out with a few ends? It's hard out in these streets," Fats stated.

Occasionally, Nigel would come through to pick Fats up and take him to one of the work sites of a house that he was rehabilitating to do odd jobs so that he could make a few dollars. He felt a sense of responsibility for his condition, given their history, even though he knew that all Fats was going to do with the money was buy more drugs. In fact, the last time he saw him a few weeks ago, he beat Nigel out of a couple hundred dollars when he begged him to pay him in advance of doing some work. When Nigel sent one of the work crew members to pick Fats up, he was nowhere to be found. Nigel wasn't upset about taking the loss. He just charged it to the disease and as a part of the game. He knew that he used to be the same way. Fats was so detached from reality, that it was clear he didn't even remember burning him for the money.

"Hop ya ass in here and let me take you to get something to eat, man," Nigel pleaded.

"Nah, I don't need food, Nigel. I need to get down, man. I'm ill and I'm trying to shake this feeling. You know how that it is, brother. Slap me with a C note. I know you got it," Fats begged.

"Here, man, take this money. I'ma do this one last time. Get some help, brother," Nigel pleaded. He reached in his wallet and pulled out a hundred dollar bill. He handed Fats the money.

His face lit up like a kid at Christmas time.

"Thanks, man. I appreciate this for real. Why don't you come thru next week and scoop me up so we can go to a meeting or something? I know I need to get myself together. Anyway, I gotta run before them boys up the hill run outta that good shit. Stay up, blood," Fats said. He jetted off on his mission of self-destruction. He had the rapid glide in his stride that dope fiends get when they knew they were about to score. Nigel just shook his head and pulled off. He was just thankful that was no longer him out there chasing the dragon.

His next stop was at Gilchrist Hospice Care. Gilchrist was the largest and most respected hospice facility in Maryland. He had to stop by and check in on his other lifelong friend, Pretty Ricky. It was sad to say that Pretty Ricky had managed to get clean from drugs for a year before he was diagnosed with stage four colon cancer. He had done several rounds of chemotherapy, but it didn't help. His condition was terminal. The best that Nigel could do was to make sure that his good friend had the best possible care in his final days. Pretty Ricky had no health insurance, so Nigel paid the full cost of his medical bills.

When he arrived at the facility to see Pretty Ricky, he was hardly recognizable. He now weighed a measly eighty-five pounds and was incoherent. Nigel knew that his old friend had no clue what was going on, but he still felt the need to make his presence known to him so that he knew someone cared. He knew that he was not long for this world. He fought back his tears and said a silent prayer for his comrade. When he was done, he left out the room feeling that he had done the best he could for him.

His next destination was at JR's car wash to get

his car cleaned and detailed. Along the way, he casually cruised through the city, making note of potential properties that he might be interested in purchasing in the near future. The sight of so many rundown and dilapidated homes and businesses made him feel depressed when he thought about how rich a tradition of prosperity these same areas of the city used to have when he was growing up. If he had his way, he would play a major role in revitalizing the look of Baltimore, one house at a time.

He pulled into the detail shop and all the young boys instantly recognized his car. They knew he was JR's father, so they gave his whip the VIP treatment. He sat in the lounge area and sipped on a cup of coffee while he waited for them to finish. When they were done, about 30 minutes later, his car looked as fresh as it did when he pulled it off the showroom floor. When he opened the car door, the sweet smell of tropical fruit greeted his nostrils pleasantly. His butter soft leather seats were stain free and well conditioned. He tipped the cats that worked on his ride, and hopped in the driver's seat to go on about his way.

As he drove down the road and listened to the smooth sounds of Kem, he noticed a cop car in his rearview mirror several cars behind him with his lights on. He pulled off the road to allow him to pass, but was surprised to see that the cop car pulled up behind him. He had no clue what he would want to pull him over for, because he wasn't speeding or violating any other traffic codes.

The officer got out and walked towards Nigel's car. Nigel remained calm because he knew he had done nothing wrong.

"Can I see your license and registration, boy?" the cocky white officer asked rudely.

"Officer, may I ask why you pulled me over?"

Nigel asked in response.

"You can't ask me a damn thing, boy. Let me see your license and registration. I'm asking the questions around here," he replied coldly.

"Absolutely, here you go," Nigel stated calmly.

To argue with the police was pointless. A black man had no wins in those situations. He simply reached into his glove compartment and pulled out the vehicle registration and his insurance card. He paid his obviously racist "boy" comments no mind, because it wouldn't be in his best interest to argue with the officer. The old Nigel would have gotten in his ass, but the new Nigel had too much to lose. Besides, he made enough money to pay the best lawyers to handle pigs like this one.

"So, what's a nigga like you doing driving a fancy car like this? What you supposed to be some kinda of big time dope boy or something?" the officer asked as he reviewed his documents.

"No, sir, I sell real estate. Are you in the market for a home? Again, what are you pulling me over for, Officer?" Nigel shot back.

He refused to feed into the officer's ignorance. He reached under his sun visor and pulled out a business card. The officer looked at the card and his whole facial expression changed when he saw Nigel's credentials. He also obviously never expected such a calm response from a Black man. But that was because he had never dealt with a boss minded brother like Nigel Hawkins before. He was forced to bow down in his presence.

"I pulled you over because a car similar to this one was reported stolen. However, all of your paperwork seems to be in order. Let me offer my apology to you, Mr. Hawkins. Have a good day," he replied and walked back to his patrol car.

"You do the same, Officer," Nigel said calmly.

The officer walked back to his car disappointed. Nigel was one less nigga that his racist ass could provoke into doing some dumb shit so he could haul him off to jail. He didn't fit the stereotype of the angry Black male. Nigel waited for a break in traffic before he pulled off, leaving the officer to revel in his stupidity.

It was shame that he had to waste time to deal with such bullshit. Racial profiling was still a serious problem for black men in particular to deal with in this society. He was used to being harassed by the police when he was breaking the law, but those days were behind him. The more some things changed, the more other things remained the same. Racism was alive and well for a Black man, regardless of your social status. He was on his way to have lunch with his mother. This story would make for great conversation over a five star meal. Despite this minor waste of his precious time, he was unbowed and undeterred in his mission to live a righteous life, regardless of what obstacles the devil put in his path.

9

Rochelle was in the kitchen cooking breakfast for Savion and Quentin. She had on her SMS audio headphones, listening to music on her Samsung Galaxy SIII android phone while she prepared scrambled eggs with cheese, turkey bacon, and pancakes for them to eat. Quentin and Savion were upstairs in their rooms playing with their toys. She planned to call them downstairs once the food was done. She was so busy jammin' to Rihanna's new single on Pandora that she didn't hear JR sneak up behind her. She was startled and jumped when he wrapped his hands around her waist. When she turned around and saw that it was him, her shocked look turned into an angry. He didn't come home last night and she was beyond livid.

"Umm, excuse me, do you live here? I don't think so, because a married man wouldn't stay out all night and leave his wife and kids home alone," Rochelle barked. She removed his hands from around her waist and took off her headphones.

JR took a step back, cracked a smile, and waited a minute to think before he responded. He knew that he was out of order for not calling her back, and to say the wrong thing would only serve to further amp Rochelle up. He knew exactly what to do to calm her down.

"Come on, baby. Please don't start with the drama

this morning. I had to go to New York for a business meeting. It got late and I stayed overnight. Don't be mad at me, love. Besides, I got something special for you," JR replied in his sexiest voice in an attempt to cover up for the lie he just told. He wasn't in New York. He and his new best friend, Molly, had spent the entire night having a sexual marathon with Roshonda at her place. Even though she was mad, she couldn't resist him when he turned the charm on or had a gift for her.

"Mmm hmm, yeah, whatever you say, JR. You went out of town for business my ass. Even if you did, you couldn't pick up the telephone at least once?" she replied. She turned back to the stove and turned off the burners because the food was done.

Poppin' Mollys had become a regular thing for JR, since that first time he tried it and liked the high intensity sex he had with Roshonda. He even convinced her to try it as well. She experienced the same spine tingling feeling he did when they got it in. JR couldn't see himself having sex without taking one now. He wanted that same high energy level sexual experience every time, but he never seemed to match that first rush he got from the first pill he took. Nonetheless, his pursuit became more vigilant over time. He had slowly become addicted to his biggest money making product. What long term effect it would have on him and his business remained to be seen.

"You're right and I'm wrong, baby. I can admit that to you. Sometimes I just get caught up and things start happening so fast, and I forget to handle my business like I know I'm supposed to do. But just know that it wasn't because of another woman. I'm done messing around, baby. I'm all yours. You and my boys mean everything to me and everything that I do is for us to keep living this boss lifestyle that we are living right now. All of this costs money, baby and I'm on a mission to keep gettin' it. I promise you, I'ma make it up to you. You're the love of my life, Rochelle Hawkins. Having you as my wife is the best thing I have ever done in my life. You're my anything and everything," JR stated.

JR pulled Rochelle towards him and planted a kiss softly on her lips. She tried to pull away, but his grasp was too strong and her lips yearned to taste his as well. The heat between them burned intensely. Rochelle wanted to stay mad at him, but her heart wouldn't allow it to happen. Hearing JR say she was his anything and everything reminded her of their wedding day. JR said those same words to her as a part of the wedding vows that he wrote. She melted the moment that he looked into her eyes and spoke those words. She was suspended in time and felt like she was the center of his universe. His words had the same effect on her today as they did back then. Her anger had subsided in an instant.

"Whatever, JR, I'm supposed to be mad at you. Don't come up in here and try to sweet talk your way out of trouble. You're still in the dog house," Rochelle stated, attempting to sound tough.

JR paid her no mind and proceeded to let his tongue have its way with her neck as he planted kisses strategically on each side. He looked down to see her derriere being cuddled by her tight little shorts as all of her thickness hung from the sides looking tasty. JR couldn't resist grabbing two hands full of her butt as he pressed his manhood up against her. It had been a minute since she gave him some, and he longed to feel the warmth between her thighs. Rochelle yearned for him just as much, but their lust would have to be put on hold for a moment. JR had something else in mind first.

"Well, I got something that will get me out of the dog house. Come take this walk with me," JR replied.

He pulled her by the hand and they walked towards the front door. JR opened the front door for her to see his surprise. Parked out front, was a brand new powder blue Jaguar with custom designed chrome wheels. The rear license tag was personalized with the phrase Money Queen written on it. Rochelle was speechless. She loved when JR surprised her with gifts because he always did things big. He handed her the keys. She ran toward it and hopped in the driver's seat. She turned around and was even more excited to see all of the shopping bags from Gucci, Michael Kors, and a host of other high-end fashion designers piled up on the back seat. JR said nothing, and just observed his Queen in her essence. He knew what to do to put a smile on her face.

"Baby, this ride is all that. This whip is hot! This is for me? And all of these clothes and shoes are just the icing on the cake! Oh shit! JR I love you! I love you! I love you!" she repeated over and over. She carefully inspected the fly interior of her new whip and was impressed. She jumped out of the car and proceeded to smother him with wet kisses on his face.

Rochelle's new car would fit in perfectly inside of their enormous garage where they kept the rest of their big boy toys. In addition to the new Jaguar and the Bentley Azzure, they also owned a Cadillac Escalade, a Lamborghini Gallardo, a BMW M3 convertible, and the crème de la crème of cars, a Rolls Royce Phantom. JR spared no expense in flaunting his wealth in the face of his competition. He loved to ride through the hood in something so fly, that dudes couldn't do a damn thing but hate, because their money wasn't long enough to afford it.

The interior of their home was just as decked out in the finest of everything. The kitchen and bathroom countertops were all custom designed European granite. The entire first floor was paved in the finest marble tile. The artwork situated throughout the house was all exclusively designed pieces, painted by some of the finest African American artists across the country. There were a total of seven bedrooms and six bathrooms in the house. There was a heated indoor pool and full-length basketball court. There was an elevator to take you between floors. The basement was JR's pleasure palace where he would entertain his top soldiers whenever they stopped by for one of his famous parties or cookouts.

The house was worth over two million dollars, but JR was able to get it for a little less than half a million dollars, thanks to Nigel finding it in a list of foreclosures that he came across. He wanted something in a price range that on paper Rochelle could afford so that it could be put in her name. He truly lived the good life. The kind of life fit for a king.

"It's nothing but the best for my baby. Come on, let's go smash that food you got in there. A nigga is hungry. Then you can take me for a ride later in that new car," he stated.

Rochelle was in a zone. His plan had worked like a charm. Rochelle was back in pocket in the good wifey role. He helped her gather up the shopping bags out of the car. They went back inside to eat. They were greeted by the sight of their two sons running swiftly down the spiraling staircase. They must have smelled the food. The boys were on their way downstairs, eager to eat some of Rochelle's good cooking.

"Daddy!" they both yelled excitedly. Quentin and Savion ran over to JR, and each wrapped themselves around one of his legs. Their grip was so strong that he couldn't move.

"What up, soldiers? Daddy missed you guys," he stated as they began to play fight.

"We missed you too. Can you come play Madden with us?" Quentin asked.

"Fa sho, if you don't mind me beating you again," JR joked.

"Daddy, I have to be honest with you. I let you win so you don't feel bad," Quentin jabbed.

He was only ten years old, but he knew the game of football as well as any sports announcer on TV. He could quote the season statistics for any of the top players off the top of his head. He was the star player on the neighborhood intramural football team for the twelve and under age group. Quentin's team won the title the last two years straight, thanks to Quentin's play as the star running back. He saw himself as being the next Ray Rice when he got older.

"We'll see about that, right Savion? Daddy is the champ, right playboy?" JR joked with his baby boy as he tossed him around like rag doll.

"Yeah, daddy is the champ. Q, you're going down!" Savion jabbed.

He loved to be up under his big brother and father. At eight years old, he was the baby of the family and used it to his advantage all the time. Whenever he was mischievous, he would flash his innocent little smile, and both JR and Rochelle would forget about what he did to get into trouble. If Quentin was the athlete of the family, then Savion was the charmer. He got all A's in school and loved going to class. He definitely didn't inherit that trait from JR or Nigel, because education was never the strong suit of either of them.

"Y'all come on and eat!" Rochelle yelled from the kitchen.

She had prepared their plates and set them all out on the fancy dining room table. The mention of food caused the Hawkins men to make a mad dash for the table. They loved to smash Rochelle's food. When they were done eating, JR went with the boys into the game room in the western wing of the seven thousand square foot mansion to play Madden as he promised. Rochelle went back outside to admire her new toy.

After several games of Madden, JR put the boys down for their midday nap. He then made his way to the master bedroom suite to spend some quality time with his wife. He had already popped two Mollys over an hour ago, so that they would have time to kick in. He planned to blow Rochelle's back out like never before. When he opened the double doors to his bedroom, he was instantly hypnotized by the sight of Rochelle laid out across their bed, adorned in a sheer aqua blue negligee set. It was trashy, yet sexy, and that's just the way he liked it. It reminded him of just how fine his woman was, and why he chose her to be the Eve to his Adam. She lay on her stomach with her nice and round backside pointed directly at him. His manhood was aroused by the magnificence of her feminine essence. He massaged his member with his left hand as it bulged up and attempted to poke its way through his jeans.

"Damn, baby, that ass is looking like right. I think you need some help with that," JR stated enthusiastically.

"This is all yours, Daddy, to do as you please with me for as long as you want," Rochelle replied like a submissive temptress.

She turned over on her back and proceeded to massage her clitoris with both hands. Her hips gyrated in tune with the eclectic sounds of The Weekend's hot new album. Her dark nipples were erect and covered with tiny goose bumps from JR's presence sending a chill up and down her spine. She continued to tantalize her wet spot with her hands, much to JR's delight.

JR pulled his Polo t-shirt over his head to expose his firm and ripped chest. He undid his belt and let his jeans drop to the floor.

As he walked towards Rochelle, each step increased his desire. He was like a pit bull being fed raw steak. He wanted nothing more than to feast on Rochelle's cleanly shaven wetness with his mouth. JR crawled onto the bed in all of his nakedness, and with careful precision, made his way between her thighs to taste her moisture. His mouth and her clit meshed together, eliciting round after round of erotic explosions as Rochelle climaxed repeatedly with each stroke of his tongue. She tasted sweeter than strawberries dipped in the finest chocolate. Her juices gushed all over the sheets like a tangerine being squeezed in his manly hands.

The thickness of his manhood was in full view for Rochelle to admire. His love tool never failed to leave her sexy ass feeling satisfied. She reached up and took all of him into her mouth, making sure that she devoured every inch. She diligently stroked and sucked her man off to the point of ejaculation within minutes. She knew exactly what it would take to make JR reach his boiling point. Even though he just came, his erection was still at full throttle. He pulled her legs apart and inserted himself inside of her slippery love canal. At the moment of penetration, Rochelle climaxed instantly.

"JR Hawkins, I love you with all of my heart and soul. Make this pussy scream your name!" she demanded with her eyes closed.

She didn't need to see a damn thing. She just

wanted to feel the constant pounding of her private parts by her man. Her body responded with orgasm after orgasm until all of her fluids were drained. She managed to open her eyes long enough to see JR reach his second orgasm. The look he had on his face when he came let her know that no bitch could please him the way that her kitten did. They made love several more times throughout the day, with each encounter more enjoyable than the one before, until finally, they both passed out from exhaustion.

Rochelle's heart was at ease. She had a brand new car and a rack of new clothes to wear. More importantly, she was snuggled up under her king with his massive arms wrapped around her. For now, all was calm and serene in the Hawkins household, and that was all that mattered to Rochelle.

JR and Rochelle slept peacefully for several hours. She lay serenely nestled in his arms, enjoying her moment of solace alone with her man. They were awoken by first the vibration, and then the sound of JR's cell phone as it rang several times. Rochelle lifted her head off his chest and gave JR a look that could cut through Teflon when he answered the call. This was supposed to be her time to spend alone with him. It was supposed to be all about her. Instead, here JR sat on the edge of the bed, engrossed heavily in conversation with Diggy about some bullshit going on in the street.

"Yo, you saw what now? Oh hell naw! Yo, all bets are off. Hold things down until I get there!" JR uttered angrily.

He slammed his cell phone on the nightstand. He turned around to see Rochelle staring at him with the saddest puppy dog eyes. She looked like she wanted to cry. JR's heart weighed heavy in his chest. He was consumed with guilt because he knew that he hadn't

been on his job as a husband lately. He knew that
Rochelle was a good woman and deserved nothing but
the best from him, not just materially, but in all ways.
He wanted to be the kind of guy that could give her all
the quality time that she deserved, but his lifestyle just
wouldn't allow that to be. He was a hustler and boss.
He had to be ready to make moves at all times. She
would just have to continue to understand, and make
adjustments in her life to suit his needs, he reasoned.

"Go ahead and say it. Baby, I gotta make a run
and take care of this business real quick. Go ahead
and say it," she stated, as if to read his mind. She had
heard that line so many times before, it was drilled in
her brain.

"Come on, baby, don't be like that. You know
you're my boo forever and a day. I just gotta go clean
up this mess that Diggy made. These fools don't know
what to do when I'm not around. I can't have them
messing up my money. As soon as I'm done, I'll be
right back and you can take me for a ride in that Jag,"
he replied.

"Yeah, whatever," she replied nonchalantly.

Rochelle lay back with her head buried in the
pillow. She knew it would be another lonely night with
just her and the boys. A part of her loved JR eternally,
while another part of her despised his neglect. She
was in a tug of war with her emotions. It was harder
than she imagined, being the wife of a drug kingpin.
At times, it crept in her head to find her a side dude to
comfort her during these lonely nights. However,
reality always brought her back to her senses. She
knew that if she did creep, JR would kill her and any
dude dumb enough to touch her, on sight. He didn't
play when it came to his boo. The thought of another
man touching Rochelle turned him into a mad man,
thirsty for blood. She remembered one time she was

out with JR and a guy made the mistake of staring at her a second too long. JR politely walked over to the poor guy and beat him up so badly that he left him with a fractured skull. JR paid the guy off so he wouldn't press charges, but the message was clear. Rochelle belonged to him for a lifetime.

JR leaned over to kiss her on the cheek, but she pulled away. He didn't have time to deal with Rochelle's emotions right now. What Diggy just told him took precedence and needed to be handled ASAP. He took a shower, dried off, and went into his room sized walk-in closet. He pulled a pair of black jeans and a black t-shirt off the rack. He put his jeans on and carried the t-shirt in his hand as he walked deeper into the closet towards the back. The back wall of his closet concealed a hidden room that was locked by a secured entrance. He punched in the code to open the steel door. This was where he kept an arsenal of weapons that made what the rapper, TI, got caught with, look like child's play.

He kept so many guns around because he had to be prepared just in case somebody was foolish enough to come after the King. JR reached up onto one of the shelves and grabbed two forty caliber Smith and Wesson handguns and several clips of ammunition. He grabbed his bulletproof vest and put it on. He pulled his black t-shirt over his head, put on his custom made double gun shoulder holster, and placed one gun on each side. Several magazines of ammunition were thrown in a black duffel bag. He headed out of the secret room, back into the main closet area. JR threw on a black jacket to conceal his weapons.

When JR returned to the bedroom, he kissed Rochelle on the cheek and jetted out the house. He jumped in the Escalade and was on his way to link up

with Diggy and the rest of his crew. The bug that
Diggy put in his ear was that somebody was out of
pocket and needed to be dealt with expeditiously. The
two guns that he was strapped with made it clear what
time it was. JR was on a mission to make his voice
heard out in the streets.

10

Nigel admired himself in the mirror once more. His tailor made tuxedo fit him perfectly. He adjusted the collar on his shirt and put on his bowtie to complete the fresh look of his ensemble. He would make a perfect candidate to be on the cover of GQ magazine. A tall, dark, and handsome black man, decked out in the finest threads would surely make the magazine fly off the shelves. Nicole was impressed as well, as she admired him from behind. The smile on her face along with the naughty thoughts in her head revealed how truly fascinated she was with the debonair black man that she called her husband. The scent of his John Varvatos cologne tantalized her desire for him even more, because there was nothing sexier than a fine brother that smelled good.

Nigel turned around and was equally enamored with Nicole's elegant black gown. She was truly a vision and blessing sent down from heaven to make his life complete. Her dress fit her body perfectly and showcased just how meticulously God had crafted her physique to be such a vision for him to enjoy at his leisure. The two of them together combined to form an unstoppable force. They were truly a power couple, like Denzel and Pauletta Washington. Their chemistry was undeniable and unbreakable. Their relationship was solid as a rock, and built to last. With beauty, brains, and wealth, their destiny was truly in their own hands.

"You're looking mighty handsome tonight, Mr. Hawkins," Nicole teased.

"Thanks, my love. You're looking quite foxy as well with your sexy self," Nigel replied. He pulled her to him and they shared a passionate kiss. The temperature in the room went up a good ten degrees from their body heat.

"Nigel Hawkins, don't start nothing you can't finish, Mister," Nicole said enticingly.

"Oh, I can finish what I started. I think you know that for sure. I'll give you a break for now. We better get going. Lucky for you, my mother is downstairs waiting on us. When we get home tonight, you're all mine," Nigel shot back with a sexy seriousness in his tone. He ran his hand across her backside.

"Watch out now! I'ma hold you to that, Mister! Let's get going. We're gonna be late if we don't hurry up," Nicole said as she put the finishing touches on her makeup. She grabbed her purse and followed Nigel out of the bedroom door.

When they made their way downstairs, they were greeted by Nigel's mother, Aileen Hawkins. Although Mama Hawkins was in her eighties, time had stood still in keeping her natural beauty intact. She had aged gracefully and maintained her smooth skin and distinct facial features. The grey streaks in her hair symbolized years of wisdom, and personified her regal nature as a true black queen. She was eloquently dressed in a stunning black dress, fit for such a royal woman. Her health, however, was another story. She suffered from diabetes and high blood pressure from all of those years of cooking and eating her own delicious signature soul food. Three years ago, she suffered a bad fall that dislocated her hip, and she now walked with a cane for support.

"Look at my baby. Nigel you look so handsome. I am so proud of you, son. Nicole, you look amazing as well. Come over here so I can get a better look at you two," Mama Hawkins said. Her face lit up with the most elated smile. Nigel and Nicole came closer to where she was seated in the family room for her to get a better view.

"Thank you, Mama Hawkins. You are looking mighty snazzy yourself. I'ma have to watch you to make sure none of these dirty old men try to hit on you tonight," Nicole joked. Mama Hawkins smiled as well. Nicole loved her mother-in-law sincerely.

"Child please, there ain't nothing no old man can do for me at my age but rub my feet and go on about his business. Shoot, if he can get down there to my feet, then you betta hope he don't get stuck down there so you'll have to pick him up off the floor," Mama Hawkins said as she chuckled. They all shared a good laugh. She had a witty sense of humor. Nigel just shook his head, because he knew his mother was off the chains.

"Come on, Mama. Let me help you to the car," Nigel interjected.

The thought of his mother being with another man besides his father made his stomach turn. He bent down so she could grab his arm. Slowly, they walked towards the garage door, en route to the car. Nicole followed right behind them. Nigel helped his mother into her seat in the back of his car. He opened the door for Nicole to get in, and shut it behind him. They had dropped Malachi off at the baby sitter earlier in the evening, because the event was strictly for adults.

They were on their way to a banquet sponsored by the Realtors Association of Maryland. It was a black tie affair. Nigel was set to be honored by his peers in the real estate field for his record level of home sales for the past year. He was expected to give an acceptance speech. This was a crowning achievement in his life. To think that this no good dope fiend had turned his life around and would now receive an award for being a respectable businessman was nothing short of amazing.

He was ,however, upset that JR was unable to attend the event with him. He wished that he could be there by his side to relish the moment. He had told him about the ceremony several times, and JR said that he would do his best to come. However, when Nigel called him the last few days to remind him, he never called back. Nigel was disappointed about his absence, but unbowed and undeterred in his mission to accept the award with pride. His hard work brought him to this point, and he would be damned if he didn't accept such worthy praise from his colleagues. He was on a natural high, feeling a euphoria that cocaine and heroin could never deliver. The good life was his new drug, and he planned to drink it in until his heart was content.

11

About thirty minutes later, they arrived at the venue. The ceremony was being held at the Hotel at Arundel Preserve. The hotel was situated in an upscale community in the Arundel Mills area outside of the city. When they pulled up at the front entrance, the valet greeted them politely and helped Mrs. Hawkins out of the vehicle. Nigel gave him the keys to park the car, and then headed inside to the event. They took the elevators to the ballroom, which was located on the second floor. Once they arrived at the event, Nigel was greeted by several of his high profile colleagues along the way. He smiled brightly as he introduced his wife and mother to them. Once inside the ballroom, they were escorted to their seats in the front as the guests of honor.

In no time at all, the ballroom was filled to maximum capacity with real estate professionals and their friends and family members. Everyone from the crowd mingled with one another and seemed to be having a genuinely good time. A nice mix of urban contemporary jazz played in the background.

After a while, the master of ceremony, Terry Pointer, got everyone's attention so that the program could begin. Mr. Pointer was a short, portly Caucasian man who loved to smoke cigars. He was also the head of the largest real estate firm in the state. Nigel and he had developed a good relationship as business colleagues over the past few years. There were also several other speakers who gave presentations about some of the groundbreaking architectural building projects that would soon be under way as a part of the urban revitalization process initiated by several major building magnates in the city. Another presenter discussed new and innovative first time homeowner programs that would be soon available to future homeowners.

After their presentations were done, it was time for Nigel to be honored. The master of ceremony quieted the crowd, so that he could properly introduce Nigel.

"Everyone, I don't want to continue to bore you with all of this business talk tonight, because I know that you all came to have a good time mingling, and to eat some good food. We just have one more speaker before we can eat. This man that I am about to introduce, I must say is an upstanding human being. I've known him for several years and watched him grow his real estate firm from a small Mom and Pop shop, into a powerhouse. Not only does he help his clients find the best houses to fit their budget, he does it in a way that makes them feel good about the whole home buying process. He treats them like they are members of the family.

"In addition to his business acumen, this man believes in giving back to the community. He generously donates money, his time, and resources to help those less fortunate, expecting nothing in return. He's real estate mogul, he's a father, a husband, and a sincere God fearing man. Ladies and gentleman, it is with great pride and pleasure that I introduce to you this year's honoree as Real Estate Professional of the Year, Mr. Nigel Hawkins," Mr. Pointer exclaimed.

The crowd responded with a deafening round of

applause for Nigel. He was in awe of the praise he received. He rose from his seat and walked towards the stage. Once at the microphone, he was overcome with butterflies in his stomach. He was nervous speaking in front of such a large crowd. He looked into the crowd at Nicole and his mother. They gave him a nod of approval, and instantly, his anxiety subsided. He gathered himself to speak.

"I just want to say thank you to you all. It is an honor and a privilege to be recognized by this organization. I am humbled, and really don't know what to say. I don't have a speech prepared, so I'ma speak from the heart. My success in this real estate business hasn't come easy. I've had my share of bumps and bruises along the way, dealing with the fluctuating equity value of homes, credit issues presented by homebuyers, to changes in the mortgage financing industry. However, some way, somehow, I managed to stay afloat. I couldn't have done it without the help of my lovely wife and business partner, Nicole. I also have to thank my beautiful mother for always believing in me and being there. Many of you don't know me personally, or know my whole story, but I'ma just put it out there.

"The man you see before you today has not always been this upstanding businessman that you see today. You see, I'ma recovering drug addict. I spent a healthy portion of my life incarcerated because of my drug addiction. I'm not ashamed to say that publicly, because I know where I've come from to get here today. I turned my life around with the help of God and the support of my family. I hope my success inspires someone else struggling with the same demons I've battled, to see that there is life after a spiritual death produced by drug abuse. I have to say that I feel good standing before you as a living testimony to God and his grace. In God's name, you can prosper in spite of your past. That's all I wanted to say. Thank you all, and enjoy the rest of the evening," Nigel testified.

His speech was met with a standing room only round of applause. He walked back to his seat, feeling on top of the world. He had climbed to the top of the mountain of success with the help of his God. Life was good. His mother's smile from ear to ear said it all. He had made her proud, after so many years of disappointment. Nothing else mattered at this point.

The waiters were very professional and attentive in promptly providing excellent service to everyone. The meal that was served was excellent. They ate a first course of Caesar salad with croutons. The main meal was filet mignon with asparagus and garlic mashed potatoes. For dessert, they were served peach cobbler. They all enjoyed the meal, and ate until they were stuffed. Nicole and Nigel shared a few slow dances to the jazz tunes that played in the background. Mrs. Hawkins just sat and watched them. She felt content, seeing her son so happy and full of life, after so many dark years. Her baby boy was now a success story. This was the perfect evening, and one to be remembered forever.

At around 11 pm, things began to wind down. Nigel said his goodbyes to everyone and escorted his mother and wife back out front to the valet section. The valet guy pulled their car up to front of the hotel. Nigel tipped the valet with a fifty-dollar bill. Nicole helped Mama Hawkins get into her seat in the rear of the vehicle. Nigel had one foot inside the car when he looked over his shoulder and noticed two white men in suits jump out of a vehicle across from them in the parking lot. They walked briskly towards them. He was caught totally off guard. He turned around to face them with a look of confusion on his face. He closed his car door so Nicole and his mother couldn't hear his conversation.

One of the men broke the silence. "Nigel Hawkins, I'm Special Agent Dick Anderson, and this is Special Agent Roger Parks. We're with the DEA. Can we have a moment of your time?" he asked calmly.

"What do you need to talk to me about? I just had one of the greatest nights of my life and you approach me about wanting to talk? I ain't broke no laws. I have nothing to talk to you about," Nigel replied sternly. His peace had been broken and he was steaming mad. Several of the event's patrons were in earshot of the conversation and whispered among themselves. Nigel felt thoroughly embarrassed. He hoped their opinion of him wouldn't be changed because of this incident.

"We can do this the easy way or the hard way, Mr. Hawkins. You can come to the station and answer a few questions voluntarily, or we can get an arrest warrant and bring you down to our office forcefully. How do you wanna handle this?" Special Agent Parks butted in.

Nigel glanced up and down at both of them. He knew he had no choice in the matter. When the Feds were involved, your options were limited. He couldn't believe this was happening to him. This was his second run-in with the law in a month. *The devil is sure nuff busy,* he thought. He had no contact with drugs whatsoever in years, so he was totally confused about this twist of events. He motioned to the agents to give him a minute as he opened the car door to speak with Nicole.

"Babes, these federal agents need to talk to me about a few things. They want me to come with them," Nigel said calmly. He didn't want make Nicole and his mother worry. He had to appear to be in control of the situation.

"Nigel, what do you mean you need to go with them, baby? You haven't done anything wrong. This has to be a mistake. Is this about JR?" she asked anxiously. Her heart raced rapidly.

Mama Hawkins sat in the backseat not knowing what to think about what was going on.

"Calm down, baby. It's no need to worry. You're right I haven't done a thing. I need you to call my brother, Albert, and tell him to meet me at the DEA office," he said, trying to further defuse the situation.

Nicole was in no mood to be handled. They were messing with her man and she was not about to sit by idly and let it go down without speaking her mind. "You're not going anywhere without me. Hell no! That is not happening! You people don't have anything else to do but harass a good man like my husband. He's a businessman. Why don't you spend your time chasing thugs in the streets?" Nicole quizzed the agents angrily. She had gotten out of the car now to make her voice heard. She looked directly at the two agents. She was dead serious about going with Nigel, and unwilling to budge in her position.

"Mr. Hawkins, you have a decision to make. What's it gonna be?" Agent Parks asked.

"My wife has made it clear she's coming with me, and my mother is almost 80 years old. What am I supposed to do, just leave her here?" Nigel asked, putting the officers on the spot.

"She can come along as well, and we will make sure that we have someone get her home safely," Agent Anderson uttered attempting to move the matter along.

"Let's get this over with as quickly as possible," Nigel said bluntly. He jumped in the car to follow the agents back to their office.

"I just can't believe this! I can't believe this! You know this has to do with your son. I told you his bad deeds were gonna come back to haunt us in some way or form. I just knew it. We've had a good night, and his crap ruined it without him even being here," Nicole rambled angrily.

"Nicole, I don't need this right now. Please be quiet. I need time to think. Just give me a minute. You bad mouthing my son is not gonna do a damn thing to help the situation. You don't know what this has to do with at all, yet you're passing judgment on JR. Get the facts first before you make those statements," he replied bitterly.

He had to remind her that she was badmouthing his flesh and blood. Truthfully, he knew this whole situation had to do with JR, but hearing the truth from Nicole right now was not what he needed. One thing he knew for sure, was that he would make no statement to them without Albert being present.

"Yeah, whatever," Nicole said coldly.

Nigel was about to respond when his mother interrupted him. "Everybody needs to just calm down, now. Let's just calm down. You two arguing ain't making this any better. Put this in God's hands. My son made me so proud tonight to see him being praised by so many people. Nigel, I have waited so many years to see you in this light. You've come too far in your life for the Lord to take you away from me now. I have no worries. Let's just let these men do their jobs and everything is going to be all right. If this has anything to do with my grandson, he'll have to answer to the man upstairs for his actions," Mama Hawkins said, attempting to defuse the tension between them before it escalated.

"You're right, Mama. We'll just have to wait and see," Nigel reasoned. He retrieved his cell phone to call his brother, Albert. He answered on the third ring.

"Hey, Nigel, what's up? Why are you calling me so late? Is everything okay? Did something happen to Mama?" he asked anxiously.

Over the past few years, they had developed a much better relationship than they had growing up. Despite his initial reservations about Nigel's commitment to change his life when he came home from jail, Albert had to bear witness to Nigel's transformation after seeing all of his business success. He was genuinely proud of his brother. His other brother, Franklin, changed his perception of him as well. They all would get together on occasion to play golf or attend church events. Mama Hawkins was happy to see her three sons have a relationship as brothers, as she had always envisioned.

"Relax, bro. Mama is fine. It's me that needs your help. I need you to meet me at the DEA's Baltimore headquarters. They say they wanna question me about some things. I need you to be there for me," Nigel replied.

"I'm on my way. We will get this all straightened out," Albert uttered.

In the past, Albert would've been skeptical about what his brother did to get the attention of law enforcement. However, being that he was a changed man, he was convinced that this had to be a mistake, or involved his nephew, JR, no doubt. He tried on several occasions to get him to sever ties with him because he knew that his shady dealings would come back to pose a problem in his life, but Nigel wouldn't listen. Nonetheless, he would be there to support his brother in whatever capacity he needed.

Nigel hung up the phone and looked at Nicole. She appeared to be livid. She was not in a mood to be reasoned with right now. He attempted to hold her hand, but she pulled away from him. They pulled up at the DEA office. Nigel was nervous because it had been so long since he'd seen the inside of any law enforcement office. The whole scene brought back memories of his past interactions with the law. He thought that was all behind him now, with all of the progress he had made in his life. Yet, here he stood; about to be interrogated about God knows what by the law. They parked in a spot and prepared to go inside. The wait would be over in a moment. All questions would soon be answered.

When it came to the Feds, they never came for you unless they had something concrete to work with from the start. Nigel put his trust in his higher power that things would go in his favor as his life, his future, and the future of his family hung in the balance.

12

When they arrived at the DEA office, Nigel parked his car in a spot adjacent to where the agents parked. He jumped out to open his mother's car door and helped her to her feet. Nicole, still steaming mad about the whole situation, got out of the car and walked with them towards the station entrance. The agents followed closely behind.

Once inside, Agent Anderson searched for one of the female agents to take Mama Hawkins home, while Agent Parks escorted Nigel and Nicole into an empty office. When he flipped the light switch on, Nigel was aghast at what he saw. He was sure that his eyes had deceived him. There were several boards on the back wall of the room, and they were littered with pictures of JR's entire organization, from the street level workers all the way up to him. He had clearly been under surveillance for quite some time, without a clue. Nicole was equally stunned by the great detail the agents had about the infrastructure of JR's organization.

"Are you surprised, Nigel? Don't be. This is only the beginning of what we want to discuss with you," Agent Anderson interjected, noting Nigel's amazement at the organizational flow chart they had on display in the room. He had successfully arranged for Nigel's mother's transport home before he joined them in the room.

"I'm not saying a thing until my attorney gets here," Nigel stated firmly.

"That's fine. Until he gets here, we'll do the talking," Agent Parks stated confidently.

"I'm listening," Nigel shot back defiantly.

"Well, let's see where do we start? As it is apparent, we know all of the key players involved in your son's drug ring. We've had wiretaps on all of his top lieutenants' phones for quite some time. It's only a matter of time before we nail them. The only thing we don't have, is proof to nail your son dead to right. That JR is a smart one. He never touches drugs or talks about it himself on the phone. It's like he manages to stay a step ahead of us all the time. However, that's where you come into the picture. With your help, I'm sure it will be a lot easier to get him to talk more open and freely," Agent Parks stated as he revealed all of the cards that the DEA had so far.

"And just why would I want to help you put my son in jail for the rest of his life?" JR asked inquisitively. He had a slight smirk on his face. *These pigs must be outta their minds if they think that I'm gonna rat on my son!* He thought. Right before the agents had a chance to respond, Albert walked into the room.

"Good evening, gentlemen. I'm Albert Hawkins and I'm here to represent my brother in this matter. Since you have not arrested him, and he came here of his own free will, I hope you have a damn good reason for subjecting my client to this undue harassment. My brother made his mistakes in the past, and paid his debt to society. Today, he is one of the finest and most respected members of the Baltimore community. This has to be some mistake," Albert stated rather bluntly and with all of his best legal prowess on display.

"You are correct. I do believe that Mr. Hawkins has done an excellent job in cleaning himself up over the years. I admire a man that can overcome a drug addiction and make something out of his life afterwards. However, would you care to explain where Mr. Hawkins got the start up money to begin his real estate business? You see, according to our sources, this money came from JR, and I think counsel, that you know the consequences of using drug money to start a legitimate business don't you?" Agent Anderson asked.

"Your sources? Would you care to elaborate on who exactly is the source of this allegation?" Albert asked. He saw Nigel squirm in his seat a little, so he knew that there had to be some level of truth to the agent's assertion. Nicole also wore a nervous look on her face as if her world was about to fall apart.

"All of that will be revealed in due time, counsel. We don't want your client. He's not the focus of our investigation. JR isn't either. We want his supplier. We want the man that's bringing these massive amounts of cocaine into the US and flooding our streets," Agent Parks stated. He pulled out a picture and showed it to Nigel and Albert.

"Who the hell is that?" Nigel asked.

"This is Julio Gomez. He is one of the Gomez brothers. This Colombian cartel is the largest supplier of cocaine to the United States. And this man right here, is one of the biggest smack importers that this country has ever seen. Yes, your son is in deep with some of the big boys, Mr. Hawkins," Agent Anderson stated.

"Not only are they heavily engaging in massive cocaine distribution in the city, but our informants also tell us that they have begun to expand into the designer drug market, flooding the streets with the new drug, Molly. We can't allow this to go on any further. Nigel, you're a man that knows the dangers of drug addiction, and appear to be a God fearing Christian. Think about all of the young kids lives that are affected by your son's criminal activities. Not only that, think about the danger that your grandkids could be in, given the company that JR keeps. Julio Gomez is not your average street dealer. He's an internationally connected player. His type does not play around," Agent Parks butted in.

Nigel felt tense and uneasy. He had made some money selling drugs in his day, but nothing on the level of what JR did today. He was amazed at how well connected his son was in the drug game. He got a clearer picture of just how much money he really was worth, and it damn near floored him. He wasn't worth hundreds of thousands, but somewhere in the tens of millions. He created this monster, and now he was being asked to bring its head to the Feds. This was one of life's cruel tricks that it played on the minds and hearts of the ones chosen to be in this position. Agent Park's appeal to his obligation as a Christian was a logical one. It was just not a valid point he wanted to hear from a pig.

"My client has no connection to these men at all. He's just an honest real estate broker, trying to live a decent life. Why drag him into this?" Albert asked.

"Because if he wore a wire, we think he can get JR to talk about his business dealings openly. In exchange for his cooperation, we won't have the IRS look deeper into his financial records to uncover the source of his original capital investment. At the time he started his business, he had no visible means of income to be able to afford to purchase several homes, let alone the money it cost to rehab them. It won't take them long to connect the dots to create an income tax evasion case against you. Nigel, think about your beautiful wife here, and your other son. They don't deserve to go through this ordeal. Make it easy on yourself. With or without you, JR is going down. You don't have to go down with him is what we're saying," Agent Parks reasoned.

"And how do you know that the funds didn't come from me?" Albert asked.

"Nice try, counsel. If you did give him the money, the IRS would be more than happy to comb through your personal and business financial records to document this exchange. If you would like for them to do that, we can set that up to corroborate your claim," Agent Anderson replied.

"I'll need some time to confer with my client. How much time do we have?" Albert asked. He wanted to help his brother out, but not at his own expense. Obviously, he had a few financial indiscretions of his own that he wanted to keep under wraps. He didn't want to draw unnecessary attention to himself from law enforcement and disrupt his happy home life.

"I understand. We know that this is a big decision. Take a few days to think it over. But I will warn you, that if your client makes any attempts to tip JR off to our operation, this deal is off the table and we will come after him with the full arm of the law," Agent Anderson threatened. It was more like a promise because he had the means to make it happen.

Albert nodded his head in confirmation of his understanding of the message being conveyed. He, Nigel, and Nicole got up and made their exit from the room. A heavy burden lay on Nigel's shoulders. On one hand, he felt an obligation to JR because he was his first-born. On the other hand, he was also obligated to Nicole and Malachi, his new family. Doing time wasn't the issue for him, because he could bit for a lifetime, if need be. He didn't want his family to be ruined financially and emotionally over JR's mess. The Feds played dirty this way to make family members turn on each other, just to get a conviction.

As Nigel walked down the hall, he happened to look into one of the interrogation rooms. He saw a familiar face that he swore he recognized as someone acquainted with his son, questioning a middle-aged White man, but he couldn't put a proper identity on the individual. Nonetheless, he had some serious choices to make. If he had stuck with his guns and not taken the money from JR, he would be in the clear. However, he did, and now here he stood in the valley of decision looking for a way out.

13

The night air outside was calm and serene, but that was soon to be replaced with fire and brimstone if JR had his way. He and his crew rode in two separate cars on their way to do what they do best, and that was to administer street justice.

Money Marvin had recently put a bug in Diggy's ear about some new cats from New Jersey that had set up shop not too far from his territory, and were making moves to cut into his business on the East side of town. He didn't have the muscle in his crew to stave off their power move, so he reached out to Diggy for JR's help. He and JR had always maintained a solid business arrangement since he took control, and he wanted things to stay that way. He copped work consistently and paid his monthly dues on time, with no issues. That alone earned him respect and suction with The Boss. He knew that if this new out of town crew continued to make inroads into his territory and cut into his business, it would mess with JR's money as well. He reasoned that JR would have no choice but to get involved in the situation to protect his own interest. Plus, everybody knew how much JR hated up North cats, after Shakim had his partner, Raynard, killed in the past. Knocking off cats from that mob would just be an added incentive for him to reinforce his position as the king on the throne.

Diggy put his ear to the streets and found out that

the New Jersey crew came from Newark, and were headed by a cat named Sheppard Pratt. Sheppard, also known as Shep, was a tall lanky light-skinned brother with dreads. He was in his late thirties, but looked to be older, due to living the hard knock life out in the streets. He had done a ten-year bid in the Feds in his early twenties, only to come home and get right back into the game with his right hand man, Jimmy Shanks.

Jimmy was of medium complexion and height, with shifty eyes and an unpredictable mean streak. He had served an eight-year stretch at Rahway state penitentiary for assault with attempt to maim. He got his name from in the joint for being surgical with how he carved a cat up with his blade. The two of them had put together a team of hungry young street level dealers that were loyal to them and serious about their paper. It was about forty of them in total. They were heavily armed with a varied assortment of high-powered weapons to ensure that if any stickup boys were foolish enough to try and hit up their stash house, they could expect to leave in a body bag. No matter how strong they were, it wouldn't matter to JR. These were his streets, and he would do whatever was necessary to maintain his regime.

Diggy and Demon ran surveillance on their operation on the low for about two weeks to learn the ins and outs on how they got down before they brought it to JR's attention. They observed how smooth their operation ran on a daily basis. They had a steady flow of traffic of junkies that came through to cop nickel and dime vials of crack rock and scrambled dope. From the looks of things, they were making major money, and none of it was being shared with JR. That was a serious problem for them, because JR aimed to monopolize the wholesale market in the city.

Diggy did his best to try to find out who their plug was, but that remained a mystery. Whoever their supplier was, had to be somebody high up on the Colombian food chain because the way the fiends kept coming back for more of their coke, it had to be cooked up something proper. Somebody moving major weight like this in Baltimore without their permission needed to be cut off at the knees before they tried to move into a position of power and threaten JR's cash flow.

Demon was able to find out that Shep and Jimmy liked to hang out at a little local spot on Milton Avenue in east Baltimore called Lulu's Sports Bar Lounge. It was a small hood joint where they would go every Friday night to shoot pool for hours, drink, and talk shit. They usually arrived at the spot around ten o'clock and stayed until the placed closed. They were always at least ten deep with a few cats being armed, just in case something popped off.

Diggy was cool with the owner's son, Rob, and he had tipped him about them being there tonight. When Diggy called JR to put him down with the situation, JR figured that this was the perfect time to pay them a visit. A surprise attack was the best approach when dealing with an unknown enemy. They would never see the ambush coming. Demon was a master of the art of delivering death and lived for these moments.

To go along for this mission, Demon recruited a handful of his best-trained soldiers. He liked to use small tactical teams to put in work, because it minimized possible casualties and left less faces that a witness could identify in a lineup if things went wrong. Roddy, Petey, Sherman, Jeremiah, and Beanie were the best of the bunch of his young cadre of soldiers. They were all hungry sharpshooters that wouldn't flinch when called upon to shed blood or lay a fool down to protect their team.

Since they were going into battle with just a few good men, against possibly a team twice their size, everything had to be carried out with pristine precision, with no room for errors. One wrong move, and they could be laid down tonight. Demon made sure they understood how crucial it was that they stuck to the plan, so nobody got hurt.

When JR heard the plan, he was eager to get in on the action. Being a boss, he rarely got his hands dirty, but there was a side to him that needed a reminder about how it felt to be in the trenches with his soldiers. It also let them know that he wasn't out of touch with the gritty side of the game, and was just as nice with them guns as he used to be. Every now and then, they needed a reminder that he was still dangerous, just in case one among them got up the courage to come for the throne.

Diggy came along because he was JR's right hand man. He had to personally make sure that nothing happened to The Boss, because he knew he wasn't ready to fill his shoes just yet. He still had a lot to learn from JR before the torch could be passed.

They were all strapped up with enough artillery to start a small war. They all also had on Kevlar vests, just in case shots were fired and somebody happened to catch a slug. As they crept slowly through the gritty Baltimore streets, JR observed anything and everything moving on each block they passed meticulously. He had run every inch of these Baltimore streets in his years. He had enough war stories to tell that he could go on for eons. This was his city, and he planned to keep it that way. The only way some Jersey cats would move him out of his spot was if he was a six feet deep. Since dying wasn't in his plans tonight, he planned to send all of them cats to hell if they didn't bow down.

When they reached the spot, Demon parked the car that contained JR and Diggy on the corner up the street from the lounge. Roddy parked the other car on the opposite side of the street on the corner. They parked on the corners, because if anything popped off and they needed to make a run, they had a clear path to the street to make a getaway. Demon surveyed the surrounding area and spotted Shep's money green colored Lexus LS 460 with the New Jersey license plates right in front of the lounge. There were two black Lexus trucks parked right behind it with New Jersey plates as well. They were all there, exactly as Rob said they would be.

JR and his gang sat outside to observe the scene and to make sure that they didn't encounter any surprises, like more members of their crew showing up unexpectedly. They also wanted to wait until the other bar patrons were gone, so that there would be no witnesses or innocent bystanders caught in the crossfire if gunplay was necessary.

They had observed several small groups of bar patrons leaving the spot at various intervals over the past hour. Diggy received a call from Rob at around midnight and he indicated that the place was empty, with the exception of Shep's crew. That was all he needed to hear. He passed the intel on to JR. It was time to get down to business.

Demon, JR, Diggy, and Petey planned to go inside the lounge. Beanie and Roddy were to remain positioned near the front door for back up, or just in case any of them fools tried to run out of the spot or they were needed for reinforcement. Sherman and Jeremiah were positioned on the corners on both sides of the street. They had a clear view of the entire block, so that they could get off clean, precise shots if any of them fools were able to make it out onto the streets. They all had the green light to shoot on sight, no questions asked. Everybody knew their role in the plan, and each one was responsible for carrying his own weight to make it go down without a flaw.

When JR and his crew walked inside the lounge, they scanned the room in search of Shep and Jimmy. Diggy spotted them in the rear of the lounge. Jimmy and Shep trash talked as they engaged in a game of pool. Rob was busy serving up a few more pitchers of beer to the rest of the crew. There were about ten other men in the vicinity of where they were located. Demon assumed that some of them were armed, and it was his intention to keep his eyes on their every movement, so that nobody got the drop on them. The four armed assassins walked towards the back as the music blasted from the speakers situated throughout the tiny lounge. When they reached the area where Shep was, JR proceeded to do his thing.

"Yo, which one of y'all dudes is Shep?" he yelled over the music. The laughter in the room stopped.

"Who wanna know, homey?" one of the men shot back.

"I do. We have some business to discuss," JR replied. The mood in the room shifted from relaxed to tense in a matter of seconds. It felt like something could jump off if the wrong thing was said by anyone.

"My man, we don't know you. I think it might be best that you and your crew move on before I take this intrusion the wrong way. We're trying to play a friendly game of pool. Clearly, you don't know who we are, or you wouldn't be here asking questions about a man that shouldn't even be on your radar," one of the men interjected.

JR didn't flinch at all. He remained calm. By the boldness of his tone, he knew that the man was Shep.

That was the only man in the room that he needed to hear from since he ran the crew. All of these other dudes didn't matter. They would all be dead anonymous John Does in a moment if they got out of line.

"You must be the one that I need to holla at, then. It seems to me that we have a misunderstanding that needs to be addressed. I'm JR Hawkins and these streets of Baltimore belong to me. No money gets made out here without my permission. However, it appears that you cats seem to think that you could set up shop here and get money without my okay. That's not how this works. East Baltimore belongs to Money Marv and his crew. They work for me. When you try to take food outta their mouths, that affects my pockets, and that's not a good thing for you. I'ma take it that you don't know any better, and give you a chance to make this right. I'ma need fifty stacks in cash by Friday for back compensation, for the time that you've been getting money out here without my consent. Also, I supply this whole city, period. If you wanna hustle here, you buy your work from me. End of story. Do we have a deal?" JR spit out without flinching. He unzipped his hoodie to reveal his two weapons.

"You're a funny guy, JR. I know who you are. We ain't paying you shit. Marvin is a bitch for running to you with his problems. You might have these other Bmore cats shook, but I'm from Newark and we don't rock like that. I got my own plug that works just fine for me. I don't need you for shit. I get money where I wanna get money, cause I'ma boss too. As a matter of fact, man you better turn your ass around and get the fuck outta here before I have my dudes here put a hole right between your eyes that'll tighten you up real quick," Shep replied with a smirk on his face.

"Yo, Shep, let me test this new Glock I just

bought, out on these fools real quick, cause motherfuckers out here are gettin' mad disrespectful. Let's see how this hot lead feels when it heat ya ass up," Jimmy threatened.

"That's the wrong answer, motherfucker. That's the wrong move!" JR shot back. These fools had sealed their own fate. There was no more room for negotiation. Death had called their name.

JR removed his guns from the holsters and took a step back. Shep looked in Jimmy's direction for a response. Jimmy went to reach for his gun, but Demon had the drop on him. Before Jimmy could let off a shot, he was greeted by two slugs to the chest from Demon's forty-five revolver. He flew backwards off the stool he was seated on. His eyes closed permanently. JR let off five shots, and three hit Shep center mass. He was dead before his body hit the ground.

A few of Shep's crew returned fire in JR's direction, but missed him as he hit the ground quickly in a defensive motion. Several shots from their guns hit Petey in the chest area, but they were caught by his vest. He was knocked to the ground from the impact of the bullets. Diggy fired return rounds at Shep's crew as a cover so they all could make their way to the front door. A couple of the men managed to escape out the lounge, only to be met by a hail of gunfire from Roddy and the others stationed outside. Dead bodies were everywhere. The room inside the lounge was smoked filled and smelled of gun smoke.

Once it cleared up, Shep and his entire crew lay dead. Rob had hid behind the bar to escape getting hit. JR's team managed to escape unharmed. They jumped in the two vehicles to exit the scene.

"We laid them motherfuckers down, dawg!" JR yelled. The adrenaline rush had him going.

Demon looked in his direction and swerved the car. The sight of blood distracted him. "JR, look at your arm, dawg" he stated nervously.

"Oh, shit, I'm hit! Fuck! I'm hit!" JR screamed frantically. Blood soaked his hoodie from the shoulder wound and continued to flow at a steady pace. He took off the hoodie and tried to use it to place pressure on the wound. In the blink of an eye, their well thought out plan had gone south. JR's fate hung in the balance. He held on for dear life, hoping that the time hadn't come for him to meet his maker.

14

"We gotta get you to the hospital, JR!" Diggy screamed frantically.

"Hell naw, I ain't going to no damn hospital. The cops will be all over my ass once this shit hits the news. Take me home. Rochelle will know what to do. She's got a doctor at the hospital that works off the books. Call Rochelle, nigga. Call my wife! Tell her I'm on my way!" JR yelled at Diggy.

He appeared to be losing consciousness from the steady blood flow. Demon put the pedal to the floor in a rush to make it to JR's estate. Diggy used his cell phone to call Rochelle. It took him forever to dial the number because his nerves were all over the place. When he finally got it right, she answered on the first ring.

"Who the hell is this calling me this time of night?" she wolfed into the phone. She sounded half asleep.

"Rochelle, this Diggy. JR has been shot! He's gonna be okay though. He got hit in the arm. I need you to stay calm," Diggy uttered.

"JR got shot? What the hell are you talking about, Diggy?" she asked in disbelief. She was wide-awake now. Her heart raced in fear. If anything happened to JR, she didn't know what she would do.

"I can't go into detail, Rochelle. He told me to tell you to call that crooked doctor you know and have him come to the house. We're on our way. We'll be there in about fifteen minutes," Diggy barked.

"I'm on it. Hurry the hell up and get him here!" she yelled before she hung up the phone.

Rochelle was a true G. She shook off her anxiety and bad nerves to take care of business. She got right on the horn and called Dr. Jasper. He was one of the attending physicians at the hospital. Dr. Jasper was a decorated surgeon with years of experience in the trauma unit. However, he also had a nasty heroin habit and gambling problem that no one knew about. A Caucasian male around five feet and seven inches tall with a medium build, you couldn't tell from his physical appearance that he was strung out, just yet. It was only a matter of time before it became apparent to the world. He was in deep to the Mob for a ton of grip, due to his vices.

Over the years, he had done countless off the books surgeries for gunshot and stab wounds for many seedy underworld figures, in exchange for forgiveness of his debts or extra side money. If you wanted to be seen by a doctor and remain off the radar, then he was the man to see. Everybody in the streets knew him well. Rochelle searched through her phone to find the number. Once she did, she got him on the phone and explained the situation. She told him she would pay him five stacks for his troubles, and he was on his way without a second thought.

While Rochelle handled business on her end, JR was fading in and out of consciousness in the car. He was losing a lot of blood and needed help badly. Diggy called Roddy and told him that JR was shot and that they needed to stop following them and ditch the car they were in. He did as he was instructed to do. After that was handled, Diggy did his best to keep JR awake by talking to him. JR's eyes closed on several occasions. He shook him several times to keep him conscious.

"Yo, JR, stay with me man. I can't afford to lose you, big brother. We got too many hoes to fuck out here, man!" he joked.

"Hell, Yeah we do. You remember that time we ran a train on them two Dominican stallions in Atlantic City? That night was live!" JR reminisced. His voice was faint, but he was holding on.

"That was a good night, dawg. I won fifty stacks at the card tables that night. You, on the other hand, lost a hundred grand, my friend," he replied.

"Oh, yeah, I forgot about that part. Fuck it. I'm rich. What's a hundred grand to a million dollar nigga like me?" JR bragged. He tried to lift his arm, but was unable to do so. He was in too much pain.

The two traded war stories back and forth for the next ten minutes, before they finally pulled up at the gated entrance to JR's crib. Demon punched in the code and the gate opened. He raced like a bat out of hell up the mile long driveway before he reached the main house. He saw a silver BMW parked outside of the house, and he surmised that it had to belong to the quack doctor, because he knew that wasn't one of JR's whips. Demon hopped out of the car to help JR make it to the house. He held him up on one side, while Diggy positioned himself on the other. They swiftly made their way to the front door. Petey took JR's house key out of his jeans pocket and opened the front door. When they entered the front door, Rochelle stood there waiting anxiously with Dr. Jasper.

"Hurry up and get him over here, now!" Rochelle barked. She wanted to fall to pieces once she saw JR drenched in blood, clinging on for dear life. She prayed to God that this wasn't his time to go. They had much more living to do together and memories to share with their kids.

"Bring him over here. Let me see what I'm working with tonight," Dr. Jasper yelled. He wiped the nervous sweat from his brow.

Demon helped JR lay down on the impromptu operating table that Dr. Jasper had set up in the large living room area. He had sheets laid out underneath it to prevent any blood from spilling on the perfectly stained hardwood floors. He had been in this situation many times before, so he was fully prepared to handle the surgery once he assessed the extent of JR's damage. He took a pair of scissors out of his medicine bag and cut off JR's shirt so that he could get a better view of his wound. He noticed that the bullet was lodged in his shoulder and surmised that it would be best to remove it to prevent it from possibly traveling through his body and causing damage to other organs.

"So what's the verdict, Doc? Is he gonna be okay?" Diggy asked. They anxiously awaited the doctor's feedback.

"He's gonna be fine. I need to get the bullet out so it won't cause any further internal injuries. Plus, I'm sure you wouldn't want it to remain in you for evidence purposes if the police question you about how this happened, right?" he asked as he looked at JR.

"Do ya thing, Doc. Handle yours," JR replied in his weakened state.

"This is gonna be painful, but I know you can handle it. Rochelle, hand me my bag. I need some Lidocaine so that I can numb the area," Dr. Jasper requested.

Rochelle handed him his bag as instructed, and Dr. Jasper went to work. He took out a small vial of Lidocaine and drew it up into a syringe. When he inserted the syringe into JR's arm, he let out a loud scream. It hurt like hell, but his pain soon turned to numbness as the drug took effect. Dr. Jasper retrieved a pair of forceps from his bag and proceeded to dig into the wound area. Blood gushed out onto the floor. The bullet was halfway lodged into JR's arm. It took him a few attempts to wiggle it free. Once he was able to dislodge it, he successfully pulled it out. He placed the bullet inside a little metal tray. Demon would make sure that the bullet was properly disposed, so that the police would never be able to find it.

Next, Dr. Jasper stitched up the wound area carefully to stop the bleeding. When he was done, he applied pressure to the wound area as he dressed it with an oversized bandage.

"Is everything okay?" Rochelle asked. She saw injuries like this countless times at work, but this was different. This was her man, the love of her life.

"Everything went well. He made it through the rough part. Now he just needs to rest for a while. I'll leave you some antibiotics for him to take, so he doesn't develop an infection. I'll also give you some Percocets to take for the pain. In a few weeks, you'll be as good as new. Rochelle will know what to do if there are any problems. You're trained for this kind of thing," he replied.

She nodded her head in agreement and exhaled.

"Thanks, Doc. You're a lifesaver. You remind me of this TV show I watched a few months ago called The Mob Doctor. It was about this white doctor that did medical stuff for the mob off the books. Yeah, that's you. I got my own mob doctor. That's some good shit right there," JR joked. He was a little groggy as he lay back on the table.

Demon and Diggy helped him sit up and to get to his feet.

"Well, now that my work is done here, there's one

more thing to handle," he hinted as he looked at
Rochelle.

"Here you go. Thanks, Dr. Jasper. I trust that this
will stay between us, correct," Rochelle quizzed. She
handed him a stack of hundred dollar bills as
promised.

"Absolutely. I wouldn't have it any other way. I
trust that you gentleman can handle cleaning up this
mess," Dr. Jasper uttered. He put the money in his
medical bag, threw the bloody towels on the floor,
folded up his surgical table, and was on his way. It had
been over three hours since his last fix and he needed
to get on. A heroin jones waited for no man.

"You need to get some rest, Boss, and lay low for a
few days until the heat dies down," Demon reasoned.

"That, my friend, is a good idea," JR agreed.

"Don't worry about a thing. We'll take care of this
mess. Rochelle take good care of the big man," Diggy
stated.

"That's my baby. I got this," Rochelle reassured
Diggy.

JR wrapped his arm around her neck and they
proceeded to walk towards the stairs.

Diggy and Demon stayed behind to clean up the
blood off the floor and to dispose of the bloody sheets.
They would retrieve JR's bloody clothes before they
left, to get rid of them as well. The guns that they used
would be buried someplace where no one would ever
find them. Demon knew that the police would be
asking questions once all those bodies were found.
Diggy assured him that Rob was solid and wouldn't
say a word about what went down. All he had to do
was say that he ducked down when the shooting
started and didn't see the shooter's faces and he would
be fine. Of course, if he did decide to tell another
story, Demon had ways to handle that situation,

should it arise.

Overall, it was a good night for them. They got rid of a potential rival, and let it be known in the streets that the Money Kings were in charge. Once JR was back to full strength, it would be back to business as usual. For now, the streets could breathe a sigh of relief.

15

"Good morning, honey," Nigel said politely.

"Mmm hmmm. It's not a good morning, as I see it," Nicole shot back coldly. She proceeded to fix herself a cup of coffee.

"Daddy, it looks like Mommy is still mad at you," Malachi interjected.

Even though he was just a child, he could sense that something was wrong between his parents. He was used to them interacting in a happy and affectionate manner, but lately they had been exchanging snide comments towards each other. What brought about this change between them baffled his young mind.

"Mommy is not mad, honey. Be careful, don't spill that orange juice on your shirt," Nicole stated, attempting to put his young mind at ease. She didn't want her issues with Nigel to have an impact on Malachi. He finished his breakfast and waited for her to gather her belongings so that she could drop him off at school.

"Mommy and Daddy love each other, son. You don't have to worry about a thing, sport," Nigel chimed in. He reached over to kiss Nicole on the cheek. She wanted to pull away from him, but opted against it because it would send the wrong message to Malachi.

Since the night of his meeting with the DEA agents, Nigel's world had been turned upside down and inside out. He and Nicole were engaged in non-stop bickering and arguing back and forth about being tangled up in JR's illegal dealings. It put a strain on their marriage and left him feeling disillusioned. He couldn't focus on the real estate business, because his home life was a wreck. The ultimatum given to him by the agents gave Nigel some serious choices to make. He had to choose between betraying his first born son or to lose both his freedom and quite possibly his family. He went back and forth in his head for the past few days to try to come up with an alternative to those choices, but he couldn't find one. When the Feds got involved, your options were limited.

He had to decide between being a snitch, by providing information to the DEA that would lead to JR going to jail, or he could stand tall like the street soldier that he used to be and tell them to go to hell. Years ago, this would've been an easy choice for him when he was running wild in the streets. He would've took his time like a true G and kept his street credibility intact. However, the problem for him now was that he was no longer that same man. Today, he was a conscious black man, living in a different world with another young son watching his every move. He didn't want to let him down like he did JR by being absent from his life, or by giving him the wrong perception of manhood to use as a guide in life. He saw how JR turned out, as a result of his example and it would kill him to see the same thing happen to Malachi.

Nigel also had a beautiful wife who loved him to death that he stood a chance to lose if he didn't decide to serve JR up to the law. Nicole was crystal clear with him where she stood on this issue. She told him to give the Feds what they wanted and let JR deal with the consequences of his actions. In her mind, he made his bed and he should be the one to suffer because of it, not them. His brother, Albert, pretty much told him the same thing, as both his brother and lawyer. He gave him a list of his limited options and the amount of time he faced if convicted. He wasn't a young man anymore. There was a big difference between doing a bid in your twenties and in your fifties. It took a lot more wear and tear on the mind and spirit of a middle-aged man than it did on a young care free and defiant street soldier. He wasn't built for the street life anymore. Nigel was now a suit and tie corporate brother.

Nicole was further convinced about her feelings towards JR when she received a call a few days ago from Rochelle, who told her that JR had been shot. In their conversation, she didn't give her any specific details about the shooting, but Nicole remembered hearing on the news recently about a multiple homicide shooting that took place in East Baltimore that appeared to be drug related. The news anchor reported that no arrests had been made, and that the police had no leads on any suspects. She put two and two together and concluded that JR was the one responsible for this tragedy and that this was how he had sustained his injury. This was just another nail in his coffin for her. She wanted him out of their lives. The sooner, the better, she reasoned, because he wasn't worth her losing her family over.

If Nigel didn't make the right decision, she had it in her mind to go to the Feds herself and help them gather whatever info they needed to put JR away for a long time. She wasn't worried about the consequences that may come if JR was to find out she ratted on him. She was just focused on preserving her family unit.

She would protect them with her life. However, she didn't sense the same conviction from Nigel at the moment.

When Nicole told Nigel the news about JR being shot, he almost lost his mind. He nearly suffered a panic attack before she calmed him down and told him that JR had survived his injury. The thought of JR dead was his worst nightmare, but he was also realistic. He was well aware that he might receive that call one day from the coroner's office to come and identify his body because he had been killed in some drug related incident. It was only so much good fortune one man could have in the drug game before the pain came down on him at some point.

JR was no different than any other drug kingpin before him. Every dog had his day of reckoning in the streets. He just prayed he didn't have to be alive to see it come to fruition. He wanted JR to live long enough to bury him, and not the other way around.

On top of having to take Nicole and Malachi into consideration, he stood to lose his brainchild, Hawkins Realty, if he didn't play ball with the Feds. It would be a travesty to see it taken from him because of one mistake he made, in taking startup money from JR. Realistically, the amount of money that JR gave him to start the business was minute compared to the amount of money he'd generated on his own, since that time. He had succeeded in becoming a titan in the real estate world. Just as JR was a king in the streets, he was a king in his world. He wasn't sure that he was ready to relinquish his throne quite yet. He had worked too hard to get there, and to let it slip away so easily seemed like such a waste.

If he was to be arrested for income tax evasion, and lose his business, he would face public embarrassment and his life would be ruined. It would be a blow that he would be hard pressed to recover from. Overcoming his drug addiction and criminal past was a lot to do once, and he wasn't sure he had the mental resolve to do it twice in one lifetime.

Not one of the real life situations that Nigel had to factor into his decision mattered to the Feds. They would use any dirty tactic available, and put the screws to whoever they could to get their man. If it meant breaking up a family or possible bloodshed in retaliation for betrayal by their informant, that was a price they were willing to pay to secure a conviction. They played just as dirty as the criminals they prosecuted. No stone was left unturned or avenue unexplored to achieve the desired end result, which was a conviction.

He was in a fucked up place. He needed to see his son to assess for himself where his head was at, and to possibly get a clearer picture of what he should do. The federal agents gave him some time to make up his mind, but he knew that they wouldn't wait forever for a response from him. If he didn't hurry up, his mind would be made up for him. Nigel needed to see JR face to face to decide if he would be able to live with turning his back on him for the good of himself and his family. Not only would he have to live with betraying JR, but he would also have to live with the impact it would have on his grandkids.

The final issue that plagued his mind was the retaliation he would face from JR's crew if they found out that he ratted on their boss. He knew that crossing JR would be a death sentence for him. If he decided to help the Feds, witness protection had to be a condition of the deal. If that wasn't on the table, all bets were off. He planned to make all of his demands clearly known the next time he met with the agents. If he was going to be used as a tool to get him, he planned to milk the situation for everything that he could, to ease his feelings of guilt.

16

In times like this, when Nigel felt stressed, the best place for him to be was at an NA meeting. Somehow, hearing the struggles and stories of other recovering addicts gave him a moment of clarity to be able to face his own dilemmas head on. It also gave him a reminder of what choice he did not want to make and that was to use drugs again to escape dealing with his problems like a man. The support and energy he received from attending meetings was vital to his sustained recovery process. He had found himself not attending daily meetings lately, but rather going no more than twice a week due to his hectic work schedule. He knew that he needed to do better. After Nicole left to take Malachi to school, he decided to make a trip into the city to attend a meeting at his NA home group.

Nigel's home group was located at his church, Temple of New Life AME church. It was a nice sized congregation with a loyal membership of approximately fifteen hundred faithful churchgoers. The church was situated in the Catonsville section of the city in a quiet residential area inhabited by middle-aged African American professionals like Nigel. After hearing his first sermon from Rev. Reid on the process of spiritual revitalization, he was so impressed that he joined the church, along with

Nicole, that very Sunday. Since then, he made sure he was there every Sunday to receive the Pastor's spiritual vitamins.

Over time, Nigel became well-known in the church community for his generous donations to help the church in its efforts to provide valuable resources to its congregation. The church facility housed an afterschool program for church members that needed childcare services adaptable to their complex work schedules. Their church also owned a soul food restaurant that was located right next door. Nigel assisted Rev. Reid with the process of purchasing the facility. His other philanthropic efforts did not go unnoticed by Rev. Reid as he recommended that Nigel be made a member of the church's board of directors. The board voted unanimously to approve his inclusion and Nigel graciously accepted the invitation.

Part of the community outreach that the church provided was to allow NA meetings to be held there. Since Nigel enjoyed the positive spiritual messages that Rev. Reid delivered every Sunday in his sermons, he decided to give the NA meeting there a try as well. Once he did, he felt comfortable interacting with the atmosphere and fellowship that he encountered, and decided to make this meeting his home group meeting location. Being able to receive spiritual empowerment and recovery support from the same place was a blessing for him.

While he drove down the road to the meeting, he noticed that there was an unmarked car behind him, attempting to follow him discreetly. Nigel might've been out of the game for years now, but having a keen eye to spot the law was one attribute that didn't just go away for an addict. Looking in his rear view mirror, he knew that it was Agents Anderson and Parks. He had noticed them several times following him since he met with them at the station. Obviously, they were trying to make sure that he didn't try to tip JR off to the fact that he was under investigation. Nigel wasn't stupid. He knew that if he did that, all bets would be off and he was headed straight to jail. That was the last place he wanted to be. He cherished his freedom too much. He continued to drive and remained calm so that they weren't the least bit aware that he had spotted them.

Nigel pulled into the church parking lot to make his way into the meeting. He was greeted by groundskeepers as he entered the facility. He walked down the hallway corridor into the medium sized room where the NA meeting was being held. Once inside, he took a seat in the rear of the room, as the place was packed to capacity. The topic of the meeting today was the power of choice. Today's guest speaker broke down the concept of how every addict, no matter where they were in their addiction, had the power to either say no or continue to use drugs. He explained that the mitigating factor in determining what choice the addict made was the value that the individual currently placed on his or her life. If the addict had reached the point that they began to see value in their existence and wanted more out of life, he would choose to not indulge further in the self-destructive cycle of addiction. Conversely, if the addict's drug use had taken such a toll on him that his self-esteem and level of self-efficacy was low, then the drug use would persist. He expounded further on how this process of choosing to make life decisions most beneficial to the user not only applied to drug use, but also to everyday life decisions. The message was one he needed to hear, given his current dilemma. It was as if God wanted him in the room today, to hear this message personally.

When the meeting was over, Nigel shook hands with other participants and made his way back to the car. Along the way, he bumped into Rev. Reid in the hallway en route to his office. The two embraced and shook hands. Nigel whispered in his ear that he would like to have a brief conversation with him about something important. Rev. Reid instructed him to follow him back to his chambers. He thought highly of Nigel, and had no problem clearing time in his busy schedule to minister to his faithful parishioner.

"Have a seat, Brother Hawkins, now tell me what's on your mind," Rev. Reid said calmly. He took a seat behind his desk. Nigel sat down in one of the chairs on the other side of his desk.

"Thank you, Reverend. I appreciate you taking the time out to meet with me. My heart is heavy today over a personal matter. I trust that our conversation will remain confidential?" Nigel asked.

"Absolutely, it will. Lay your burden on me, my brother," Rev. Reid replied.

Nigel admired Rev. Reid's meek and humble demeanor. He loved how down to earth he was, because it made it easy and comfortable to talk with him about almost anything. He just hoped that he maintained that same open minded mentality once Nigel broke down his situation to him.

"Well, pastor, as you know, I have an older son, JR, who is heavily involved in the drug game. Well, even though he is engaged in unrighteous behavior, he is still my son and I love him the same. Recently, I was approached by federal agents about his activities and they are applying pressure on me to try and get him to incriminate himself so that they can arrest him. They have me between a rock and a hard place. I made a mistake in accepting money from him years ago to start my business, and now they are using that against me. I just don't know what to do," Nigel explained.

"Well, I can certainly see how this is a crisis for you. However, the choice you have to make is simple. Your son is a grown man, and has made his own path in life. I know that because of your past that you feel guilt for his actions and behaviors. However, there comes a point where we all have to make decisions that are unfavorable decisions for others, but prove to be the right thing to do for our own peace of mind. I understand that you may have made a mistake taking money from him, but I believe that your heart was in the right place. We all fall short in the glory of God, but if we remain steadfast, he forgives us all. Remove this burden from your life and do what's right for young Malachi and that lovely wife of yours.

You've done the best you can for JR, in trying to offer him an alternative to his current way of life. He has to shoulder the burden of God's judgment for his actions himself. Free your spirit of that obligation. I'm not telling you something that you don't already know in your heart," Rev. Reid ministered to Nigel. It was as though he could read his subconscious mind.

Nigel just nodded his head in agreement. What the minister said was the uncut truth. He already heard the same thing from Nicole and his brother, Albert. He got up from his chair and embraced Rev. Reid. As he made his way to his car, he spotted the agents parked on the other side of the parking lot and walked towards them. He didn't care any longer, if they knew he was on to them. When he got near the car, he motioned for one of them to roll down the car window. Agent Anderson obliged him.

"Ok, I'll do what you want, but I'll need full immunity from prosecution and witness protection for me and my family," Nigel said frankly.

"That's a done deal. I'll get the paperwork drawn

up for you to sign," Agent Anderson stated without hesitation. A smile of approval came across his face.

Nigel walked back to his car. He was uncertain, but optimistic that he had made the right choice to become a cooperating witness against JR. His decision went against the code of the streets that he was raised to live by, but he didn't care any longer. He wanted to save his family and the financial empire that he created. Even though he would have a new life and new identity, he planned to come away with a good portion of the money that he had made in the real estate business to live off comfortably for many years to come. He didn't care about his street credibility being destroyed, because he was no longer about that life. He might have been considered a rat or snitch by the streets, but in his mind, he was a responsible father and husband, and no longer a thug. He gave the streets over thirty plus years of his life and they gave him nothing back in return but misery and wasted time. He owed them nothing.

He did owe Nicole and Malachi everything, because they were his new life source. He made his way home to tell Nicole his decision. He knew that she would be relieved that he finally saw things from her perspective. He thought about the impact his decision would have on his mother and his brothers. Once he was in witness protection, he would never see them again. The sad reality tore at his heartstrings. He had worked so many years to regain their trust and to build a healthy relationship as a family, and now it would be all for naught. His heart pounded rapidly and was filled with grief. He never imagined that taking money from JR could affect his life on so many levels. Hindsight was 20/20 vision. He had to accept his decision and bite the bullet on this one.

From this point on, his life would never be the

same. He put his entire faith in the same legal system that he spent a good portion of his life defying. He would need every bit of their help and protection once JR found out about his betrayal. He would be a man marked for death with a bounty on his head. He knew this to be true, because if he were in JR's frame of mind and facing the same circumstances, he would do the same thing. Only God could comfort Nigel's troubled soul. His freedom was a bittersweet compensation package for the pending loss of his first-born, his mother, and his brothers from his life. The weight of the world rested on his shoulders. He prayed for the strength to endure and carry the load.

17

"This case is coming together perfectly, partner. I think this time we are gonna nail these drug dealing niggas to the cross for good," Agent Anderson said with a cocky swagger. He damn near pissed in his pants because he was so elated. He couldn't contain his jovial spirit.

"I agree. The pieces are falling right into place. It's only a matter of time before they start to turn on each other. One thing that's different about these niggas in the underworld that's different from the Italians. They will sell each other out at the drop of a dime to save their own ass. They have no honor. You hear them in those rap songs saying that it's ride or die and speak about having loyalty for your team, but that's the biggest crock of shit. You dangle a sweet enough carrot in their faces and they will sell their mommas out in a heartbeat," Agent Parks said in corroboration with his partner's racist rant.

"It works just like that almost all of the time. Hey, who am I to complain? It works in our favor and makes us look good. Once we bring this one home, this case is gonna definitely help us make a name for ourselves in the agency. I can see promotions for the both of us coming in the near future," Agent Anderson envisioned.

Parks nodded his head in agreement. He shared the same vision.

The two agents drove back to the station, admiring their crafty handy work. They were proud of the fact that they were successful in applying pressure to Nigel to get him to flip on JR and help them build their case. It didn't matter to them that they had broken a bond between father and son, as long as they got their man. Obtaining convictions and long prison sentences was the goal of every federal investigation, and they did so by any means necessary. They would lie, manipulate, plant evidence, and even threaten to separate parents from their children to convince or coerce a target to cooperate as a witness in an open investigation. Sometimes, however, these tactics don't always work to the degree that they play them to and things go awry. Such was the case a few years back for the DEA, when they went after one of the biggest drug cartels in Baltimore City history.

Both agents were involved in the federal investigation of the infamous DFL drug crew that ran the drug game in Baltimore nearly a decade ago. They carried a grudge that they were unable to make that operation as successful as it should have been. They didn't move fast enough on leads when they came up, and failed to follow up on others that they should have. Although the crew was dismantled, thanks to testimony from a few key players and the death of one of their leaders, Tyrone Waters. The remaining top lieutenants all received prison sentences of less than twenty years. They would live to see the streets again. In addition to the short prison sentences that were handed out, the other leader of the DFL crew, Dayvon Freeman, still eluded capture and he was still a wanted fugitive. To this day, they don't know how he got away, and they will not rest until he is captured.

They would be sure not to make the same mistake this time. JR Hawkins was a marked man, living on borrowed time, in their books. He was going down, even if meant him being toe tagged in a body bag. His fate was sealed as far as they were concerned. They planned to use his capture as major coup in the agency. This would be their career defining case. If they got JR and the Gomez Brothers in one sweep, they would be national heroes in the war on drugs. The keys to the kingdom of career upward mobility would be at their feet. Every agent lived to have this kind of suction and leverage with the top-level administration.

"Can't you just see the look of shock on this JR character's face when he looks across the courtroom to see his own father on the witness stand testifying against him in open court? We got a notorious, long bidding Baltimore gangster to turn into a CI. Man this case is a slam dunk!" Parks jabbered on.

"JR is big fish to catch indeed, but let's not lose focus on the real big fish here. I want Julio Gomez. These big time Colombians get away from us every time and they laugh in our faces. The bosses always cave in to international political pressure from these damn foreign diplomats that protect these death dealing maggots in exchange for their money. Man, this shit makes me sick," Anderson said angrily.

The Gomez brothers had been on the DEA's list of international targets for over fifteen years. They were one of Colombia's longest standing criminal cartels in existence. Julio Gomez was so successful in keeping the top leadership of the cartel out of harm's way from law enforcement for numerous reasons. First of all, he was one helluva diplomatic negotiator and businessman. He was successful in brokering a peace treaty with other competing cartels in Colombia to forge a united front against Colombian and American law enforcement, so that they all could stay in business. His rationale was that if the cartels continued to fight each other over control of the cocaine trade, it left room for law enforcement to eventually annihilate them all, one by one, over time. However, if they all forged a united front and worked together for a common cause, there was no way for law enforcement to infiltrate their wall of solidarity, as long as they adhered to the established guidelines. He believed in the concept that there was greater strength in numbers than in the efforts of splinter organizations going up against the Colombian police department, backed by the efforts of the United States government. That would be a war that each of them would eventually lose over time.

The first guiding principle for the mutually beneficial pact between the families was that each cartel family would have to agree to not make efforts to seize control of the territory operated by another crime family. He reasoned that this would only lead to unnecessary bloodshed and loss of crucial personnel. Colombia had a rich history of cartel related violence that reached up to the highest levels of government. All of the bloodshed, while sending the message clearly to the regular citizens that it was dangerous to cross these entities, drew nothing but negative international attention to the activities of these crime families, and served to strengthen the negative perception of them in the public eye. This negative attention, in turn, gave law enforcement a green light to go after them with increased vigor to bring an end to these bloodthirsty gangs of drug dealing killers. However, if the bloodshed decreased, it gave them the opportunity to spin the public outcry for their heads into one of them being seen as the victims of undue harassment by law enforcement.

To further spin the public perception of their

organizations, Julio argued that each cartel would have to increase its efforts to provide necessary financial and social resources to the poor, indigent residents that lived in their territories. They would need to establish social programs that provided food, clothing, and shelter to help increase the resident's standard of living. They would need to finance legitimate businesses in the names of law-abiding citizens to create jobs for the unemployed and uneducated masses of the population.

Julio argued that if they empowered the common people with a means to provide for themselves and their families, they would be seen as heroes and not villains in the communities. With the backing of the people, law enforcement would be at a stalemate in finding corroborating witnesses to come against them. They would all be viewed as victims of oppression, who utilized the resources they had available to them, that being cocaine, to acquire wealth, so that they could help their poor brethren maintain a decent standard of living that the Colombian government failed to provide. The people would hail these cartels that were once seen as evil empires as Robin Hood figures that stood for the uplifting of the disenfranchised masses of the Colombian people. Once he got the other cartels on board with his plan, their solidarity, combined with the support of the people, made them untouchable inside the walls of Colombia.

The third factor that made Julio such a visionary and brilliant organizer was his ability to have virtually every high ranking political figure in Colombia on his payroll. He knew that all public figures had some dirt or indiscretions from their past that they wished to remain hidden. He did his research and utilized his vast financial resources to uncover these dirty deeds to blackmail them all to go along with his scheme. He had them all in his hip pocket, and at his disposal to provide whatever assistance he needed to maintain his organization. Any political investigation into his organization was squashed before it got started. Truth be told, he was the real President of Colombia behind the scenes, because he had the power to make anything happen at any time.

For them to bring down a man as powerful as Julio Gomez, it would take a carefully laid out plan and some heavyweight American political influence to back their investigation into the drug organization. Parks and Anderson did their own legwork outside of the DEA in contacting a well-respected and influential politician who had the international power and influence to usurp the authority of the Colombian officials that backed the Gomez brothers in bringing them to justice if the evidence he had was compelling enough to demand such action.

Senator Paul Connors from Texas was the man to give life to their career case. Before he became a politician, he was a wealthy oil tycoon with widespread international connections. He also had two children that died from drug overdoses. Their deaths inspired him to become an outspoken advocate for stiffer sentencing and punishment for drug traffickers. He didn't believe in going after the street level dealers or the helpless drug addicts. He was bold, brash, and cocky enough to want to go after the organizations like the Gomez brothers, because they were responsible for bringing the drugs into the United States.

When the agents interrupted him one day at a golf game at his hometown country club to talk to him about their ongoing investigation of Julio Gomez, he was all ears. He was impressed by what they had gathered thus far, but informed them that he needed a stronger case with no flaws, in order to use his influence to cut through the political red tape and barriers to get the brothers extradited to the United States to face charges for importing drugs into the country. Once they heard this, the agents went to work, and were now at the breaking point of the investigation. They had to get JR on board to make it all fall right into place.

"Me too, my friend, I'm just as disgusted as you are with these bastards. JR is the only one in a position to give us information to nail Julio dead to right, because he had direct dealings with him. Flipping him is gonna be one helluva job, but I think we can pull it off. He's rock solid, but every man has a breaking point. We've got his father in place, and our guy inside his organization giving us good intel, but that's not enough to make him crack. I've got one more angle to work that I think will force him to turn," Parks said optimistically.

"I'm glad you thought of this option. It's worth a shot. Pull over here. There's the truck we're looking for right there," Anderson instructed.

Parks pulled the sedan next to the truck and Anderson got out of the vehicle. He had a large manila envelope in his hand. He looked around to make sure that no one was around in the parking lot, and placed the envelope underneath the windshield wiper. They had timed things perfectly, because they had watched their target's habits for the past week. They were sure that the recipient of the package would be along soon to retrieve it as expected. They pulled the car over to a remote location and waited for the person to arrive.

In about fifteen minutes, the person arrived like clockwork. They noticed the envelope on the windshield, retrieved it, and got in the truck to drive away. Once the person was gone, Parks and Anderson pulled off as well, on their way back to the office to await a phone call, because they were sure that the information contained in the package would elicit one.

18

Nigel sat outside of JR's home for a few minutes with a slew of rambled thoughts rattling around in his brain. He had butterflies in his stomach. His palms were sweaty. That vein that popped out in his neck whenever he was nervous was clearly visible. He told himself that he just needed to relax and get this over with as soon as possible. There was no time for second guessing. He had made his decision and had to live with his choice. At this point, he was in too deep to turn back now. The job had to be done. He mustered up the resolve to ring the doorbell. Rochelle came to the door with Quentin and Savion right by her side. They were eager to see their grandfather, whom they affectionately called Pop Pop. It had been a minute since PopPop had come to visit them.

"Hey, daughter in law, how have you been? You're looking beautiful as ever," Nigel stated as they embraced.

"I'm good. I can't complain at all. Of course, taking care of that stubborn son of yours is no easy job, but I'm still here. You know these two little munchkins are so happy to see you," Rochelle replied.

"Pop Pop, I missed you," Quentin stated as he gave Nigel a big hug.

"Yeah, we missed you, Pop Pop. Look at what Daddy bought me," Savion stated as he hugged Nigel as well. JR had bought him a puppy recently, because he had begged for one for so long. He was a baby pit bull that he named Chopper because of his razor sharp teeth. Chopper ran into the room and rubbed up against Nigel's leg. Nigel bent down and stroked his back.

"Granddaddy's boys are getting so big. Look at you both looking just like your daddy," Nigel stated with big smile on his face.

He wished that he had spent more time with his grandkids. Seeing them made him realize how much they meant to him. It also made him realize how it would tear them apart if he played a role in taking their father away. He wished he could make this moment last forever because this would probably be one of the last times that he saw them. He wanted every second to last forever, as he drank in every one of their unique facial features and mannerisms. He would miss them immensely once he went into witness protection.

Nigel played with the boys for a few moments more before Rochelle led him down to the basement area where JR was in the theater room watching a documentary about the DFL crew, one of Baltimore's most notorious crime families. JR loved the movie so much, because he came up in the game at the time when the DFL crew ran things on the streets. It represented a graphic portrayal of the mean Baltimore city streets that he knew so well. The DFL cats were hustlers that he looked up to and aspired to be like. In fact, he modeled the Money Kings after how Dayvon and Ty had set up the structural framework of their team. Never did he imagine that his arm in the game would surpass theirs by leaps and bounds.

While they were local legends, thanks to Julio, JR was now affiliated with an international cartel. He had a direct link to one of the biggest, if not the largest plug in the country. He took the game to another level.

When Nigel walked in the theater room, he was seated on the couch, chillaxing as he continued his recovery from being shot. His arm was elevated inside of a sling. He was still in some pain, but the worst part was over. Now, it was just a matter of time before he was back to normal and able to have full, functional usage of his arm.

"Hey, son, what the hell happened to you? How in the world did you get yourself shot?" Nigel asked as he observed the sling on his arm. It was his first time seeing him since the shooting.

"It's nothing heavy, Pops. I had to show these fools that I'm the boss around here. Some Jersey cats tried to mess with my money, and had to get dealt with Bmore style," JR bragged.

"So that was you and your boys involved in that shooting that's been all over the news?" Nigel asked.

"Yup, and it felt good to be in the mix. I haven't put in any work in a while," JR replied proudly.

"You mean to tell me that you got shot because you put yourself in harm's way over a turf beef? Son, I'm surprised at you. You're supposed to be a boss in your crew, not a foot soldier. When you're on a certain level in the drug game, you don't get your hands dirty anymore. You delegate that to your workers. That's what you pay them for, to handle things on the front line. You're supposed to be in a position now to run things behind the scenes. That was hustling 101, which I taught you. You must've not been paying attention," Nigel spit out. He took a seat in one of the leather theater chairs. He reminded JR about some of the heavy OG street law he used to lay on him as a child. Even though he was out of the game, he found himself reminiscing momentarily about how he handled business in his heyday. He snapped himself back to reality because he had a job to do.

"I hear you, Pops, but sometimes I like to get my hands dirty. When I pulled that trigger and watched that fool squeal like a little girl after talking trash to me, I felt alive. Besides, he disrespected the king and he had to be punished. I wanted to look that fool in his eyes so that his last image would be mine," JR replied cockily.

"JR, I can't deny it. You are truly my son. That's something I woulda said back in the day when I was in the game. At least you got that swagger honestly," Nigel joked. He did his best to make JR feel at ease, so that he would keep talking.

"Yeah, Pops, we're birds of feather. So how's my little brother?" JR asked.

"He's doing great. He asks about you all the time. Man, I'm just glad you're okay. I don't know what I would've done if something happened to you," JR said honestly. He was consumed with guilt. He wanted to back out of this whole thing, but he couldn't.

"I'm a soldier, Pops. I'm built for these streets. They can't do nothing with me out here. I'ma problem for these fools," JR bragged.

"Ok, soldier. I hear you. I'm just curious and this may sound crazy coming from me, but how are you able to maintain control over all of the cocaine and heroin distribution in the city? I mean, when I was in the game, I did my thing and made a lotta money, but I always had competition out there that did their thing as well. With you, it seems like you just cleared the slate and got everybody working for you. You have no competition, and it looks like everybody answers to you. What do you have that the other hustlers don't?" Nigel inquired.

JR had a puzzled look on his face. The question threw him off guard and he started not to respond. Nigel never asked him about his business or activities. He had made it clear to JR that he wanted no parts of his street life at any time. However, since it was his father, he gave him the most honest response that he could. Besides, he wouldn't dare miss out on an opportunity to brag about his strangle hold on the drug trade.

"It's just simple math, Pops. All of the numbers add up in my favor. You're a businessman, so I'm sure you can follow me on this one. I got the best product at the cheapest prices, so why wouldn't they buy from me?" JR shot back in response.

"So you mean to tell me that all of the other wholesalers just let you lock the market down without a fight? Come on, son, it can't be that easy," Nigel stated in disbelief.

"Yeah, it is that easy. Straight like that. They can't compete with my prices. And besides, if anybody did try to take away my clientele, I got enough soldiers on deck to squash any resistance. I took this game to another level, Pops. Nobody in the history of the drug game in Bmore has gone as high up on the food chain as I am now. I stand alone in my own lane," JR said boldly. He spoke the truth. When it came to competition for him, there was none. He was the head honcho in charge. He made things move, when he wanted and how he wanted... period.

"Well, if your prices are that low to lock everything down, then you must be plugged in directly to the Colombians, huh?" Nigel asked further.

"True indeed, I am. I meet directly with the man himself. He gave me the keys to whatever I wanted and need. Since Pablo Escobar, he's the biggest there is, hands down," JR boasted.

JR normally wasn't this loose in discussing his organization, but a combination of the Oxycontin and the Molly pills made him feel super relaxed and at ease. Besides, Nigel was his father and not just some dude on the streets fishing for info. He felt that he could trust him to keep their conversation between them. At least, that's what he thought. However, Nigel had an agenda of his own.

"Who is your connect? Is it somebody that I've seen on TV before?" Nigel asked, digging deeper for more details.

"I'll just say his name is Julio. That's all I can tell you because anything else and I'll have to kill ya," JR joked. Nigel laughed as well.

"Son, while I don't condone your lifestyle, I must say that you have taken this drug game all the way to the top. I never envisioned my lessons would take you this far. But I have to ask you, how much power is enough? When do you give the game up and say that I have enough money?" Nigel asked bluntly.

"There's no such thing as enough power in this world we live in. I'm always on the hunt for more," JR responded.

"I mean, there has to be some limit to this thing for you. How much would you say you're worth, honestly?" Nigel asked.

"Honestly, I would have to say at least $25 million," JR stated without hesitation. That was just a ballpark figure. With all of his business investments at peak return levels, and the Molly drug market booming like it was, that figure would surely double, sooner than later.

"Damn, son. Are you serious? That's the kinda money that makes even a religious man like me think about making a career change," Nigel joked.

"Well, Pops, there's room for you on my team.

Two Hawkins men united in these streets, man the world could be ours," JR envisioned. He was dead serious. He would love to have his father in his corner to help him run his empire. It would fulfill his ultimate dream of the two of them together making infamous history.

"Nah, that life is all behind me now. I'ma changed man. I don't have another run in me, son. I'm happy with the money I make in real estate," Nigel replied, crushing JR's fantasy Dream Team idea.

"How much did you make in profits last year?" JR asked.

"I would say roughly around two million," Nigel replied. His profits paled in comparison to JR's fortune, but it was nothing to dismiss. Most people would be happy with a fraction of Nigel's profits.

"That's not bad at all. And to think it all started from that fifty grand I gave you. Pops, you're talking about me, but that's a major come up you made, man. I'm proud of you," JR said sincerely. He was glad to see his father being such a success after seeing him in harsher times in the past.

"Thanks, son, I needed to hear that from you. No matter what decisions you make in life, I accept you for who you are. Always remember that. I love you unconditionally," Nigel stated. He felt like shit for what he was about to do.

"I love you too, Pops. Man, that's enough of that mushy stuff. Hawkins men are soldiers. We don't get emotional," JR joked.

"Yeah, you're right. That was my bad. Well, unlike you, some of us have to work in an actual office to earn our money, Mr. Big Shot. I just wanted to stop by and holla at you for a few to see how you were doing. I've got to go into the office to close out a few deals," Nigel stated.

"Aight, Pops, be safe out there," JR uttered.

Nigel got up off the couch and bent down to embrace JR.

Before he left, he said his goodbyes to Rochelle and the kids. They had no clue that his goodbye might be a permanent one for him. When he reached his car, he opened up his shirt and ripped off the wire that was taped to his chest. JR had given him some good incriminating evidence to turn into the DEA. He hoped that this was enough to end his involvement in their case against JR. He wasn't sure that he could play JR like that again without him getting suspicious.

As he drove off, tears formed in his eyes. He was overcome with emotion because he had done the unthinkable. His father surely was turning over in his grave at the thought that the son he raised to be a G and a soldier had turned into a federal informant.

19

Sherman brought the ball up to the half court line gracefully like he was made to play the point guard position. He did a spin move and dribbled the ball behind his back to avoid the oncoming defender. Once in the clear, he passed the ball to Roddy, who was positioned outside the three-point line. Roddy dribbled the ball between his legs twice and did a jab step move that caught the player who was guarding him off guard as he maneuvered by him. On his way to the basket, he did a sweet crossover move that left another defender frozen in his tracks. By the time he recovered, Roddy was already halfway down the lane, about to lay in a sweet finger roll over top of the six foot six inch defender from the opposing team. The ball swished through the net for two points.

"Yeah, that's right, in your face, fool. What you gonna do, huh?" Roddy said emphatically as he turned around and grimaced in the defender's face to taunt him.

"Man, whatever. Just play ball," the defender replied.

He wanted to beat the dog shit out of Roddy, but he knew better. Striking another player would result in him getting a technical foul, and he knew that was not what his team needed from him at this critical juncture in the game. Roddy had been talking trash to him all game long, but he never fed into his mind games. Instead of going back and forth with him verbally, he let his game on the court do the talking for him as he maintained his focus. Besides, if he even thought about swinging on Roddy, the Money Kings goons would be all over his ass. They were deep in the crowd and made their presence known.

Instead of acting on his gut instinct and punching Roddy in the face, he took Roddy's taunts on the chin and kept his head in the game. He made his way up the court without even a glance in Roddy's direction. Being ignored only fueled Roddy's growing rage.

The player on the other team that Roddy taunted happened to be one of the top college basketball players in the country. His name was Shawn Dandridge and he was the starting small forward for the University of Maryland Terrapins. This past year, he led the team in scoring and rebounding, and was second in assists. He had the ball handling skills and jump shot of a shooting guard with a quick first step like Bernard King that made him deadly from the three position as a post up player. This past season, he was named to the All-ACC first team, and was a unanimous choice for freshman of the year. He was definitely a player being watched closely by NBA scouts, even though his game had yet to reach full maturity.

A Baltimore native, he was a star high school player at nationally recognized Dunbar Senior High School. Hundreds of college teams had offered him athletic scholarships in his senior year. He turned down schools like Duke, Indiana, Arizona, and Florida because he wanted to stay close to home to be near his family. He also chose to go to the University of Maryland, because his idol growing up was Baltimore native, Juan Dixon. He wanted to follow in his footsteps, in leading the Terrapins to a national championship like he did. With the breakout freshman season he just had, a national title was definitely a possibility in the near future for the school, as long as he continued to improve his game.

Shawn and Roddy had a history of run-ins with each other through the years. They both grew up in the same East Baltimore neighborhood across the street from each other. They played in several inner city summer basketball leagues for rival teams growing up. Their battles on the court were legendary, with each one getting the better of the other one on different occasions. Shawn, with his clean cut image, was always the crowd favorite, while Roddy was viewed as the bad boy thug who got little praise, despite his high skill level. He was also known as a hotheaded player who could be taken out of his rhythm on the court easily. Deep down inside, Roddy was envious of Shawn's success, and wanted nothing more than to have the pleasure of beating him today so that he could rub it in his face. He always felt that he was just as good, if not better, a player, and tonight was a chance for him to prove it against the city's golden boy.

While Shawn made the transition from prep school superstar and local sports hero to playing college basketball and was on his way to becoming a future NBA star, Roddy had a reputation in the city as a playground legend on the basketball court. He was known for his speed and flashy moves when driving to the hoop. He had a wicked crossover dribble that rivaled Allen Iverson's in his prime. He also had a soft feathery touch on his jump shot. He too had played basketball at Dunbar High School on the same team with Shawn. Standing six feet two inches tall, Roddy made history at Dunbar for being considered the second best point guard to ever play for the school next to the legendary Skip Wise. However, his hoop dreams ended when he got involved in the drug game at the age of sixteen.

Just like Skip Wise, he answered the call of the allure of the fast money offered by the streets and never looked back. Basketball was no longer his focal point in life. Selling crack cocaine, getting money, sexing any woman he wanted, and street credibility became his new aspirations for success in life. Nonetheless, he still loved to break ankles on the court in his spare time.

Sherman was a pretty good ball player, himself. He played basketball for Forest Park Senior High School at the point guard position. He was a solid defender with good ball handling skills. He played the game within the team ball concept and showed good court field generalship when he was on the floor. His skills were good enough to make him a three-year starter in high school, but his lack of speed and inconsistent jump shot made his college scholarship offers limited to only local schools like Morgan State University and Coppin State University. Knowing that the NBA was not in his future, he chose to hit the block and get money.

"Come on y'all. Let's D these fools up! Let's close this game out!" Shawn yelled to the rest of the team. He trotted back up to the other end of the court to play defense.

Every other Thursday, Roddy and Sherman, along with several of the other young guns in the Money Kings crew got together at Webster M. Kendrick Recreation Center in West Baltimore to run a few games of full court basketball against teams put together by some of the rival drug bosses in an unofficial basketball league. They played against some of the top local college and high school players in the city, and usually held their own. There were four teams scheduled to play two games back to back each week. Each game consisted of four six-minute quarters with a fifteen-minute halftime break in between. They hired referees to call fouls, had an official timekeeper, and even installed a digital scoreboard to make the games appear as authentic as possible.

The winning team in the two games played in a final game for the twenty five thousand dollar grand prize that was to be split up between the team members. The prize money had to be paid by the hustler who had chosen to sponsor the losing team that played in the final game. JR, via G Money, would have to kick out the twenty-five stacks if the team he sponsored lost.

In addition to the prize money, all of the top bosses made their own wagers with each other on whatever team they thought was going to win the final game. JR had a hundred grand on the line, and he hated to lose.

Early in the night, Roddy's team beat their first opponent by twenty points in a blowout contest. Roddy led his team to victory by scoring thirty-three of his team's seventy points. Sherman scored ten points and handed out seven assists. Shawn's squad also had their way with their first opponent for the first half before they had to hold on in the second half after squandering a fifteen-point lead. Not to be outdone, he scored forty points to lead his crew to victory. After a brief rest, the stage was set for the two bitter rivals to meet in the grand finale with the winner earning bragging rights and a hefty cash prize.

In the first half, Roddy and Shawn went at it, trading baskets back to back, much to the entertainment of the crowd. The score between the two teams was deadlocked at halftime at forty-two. In the third quarter, Roddy's team started to pull away as they built a ten point lead, only to have it cut to three by the end of the quarter. With two minutes remaining, the score was tied at sixty-eight after Roddy's last basket. It was clutch time, and the game was anybody's to have. This was a test of wills, whereby only the more resilient and hungry would walk away with the victory and the big pot of money to revel in afterwards.

The point guard on Shawn's team called out a play from the top of the key. Roddy moved along the baseline in an attempt to shake his defender. Once he was free, the point guard passed him the ball. He dribbled past his defender and picked up his handle to attempt a jump shot. Roddy came out of nowhere to block his shot, but Shawn managed to retrieve the ball afterwards and darted past Roddy towards the basket for a layup to tie the game. He turned around and smiled in Roddy's face as he handed him the ball to take it out of bounds. Roddy was steaming mad. The teams exchanged baskets on the next two possessions, so the game remained tied.

As time ran out, Roddy inbounded the ball to Sherman, so that he could bring the ball up court. Once they crossed the half court line, he shot Sherman a look that indicated that he wanted the ball in his hands now. Sherman passed him the ball and sprinted to the other side of the court. The clock continued to run down. There were only thirty seconds left in the game. Roddy planned to run the clock down as close to zero as possible before he took what he hoped would be the game winning shot.

He called out to his team for them to clear out the lane to make way for his grand finale. Since Shawn was the best defender on his team, he took on the assignment of defending Roddy. The two childhood rivals were now face to face in crunch time, in a battle for supremacy on the court. Neither player could have scripted a better ending. This was the kind of situation from which playground legends were born.

Roddy made a move to his left in an attempt to shake Shawn, but he remained stuck to him like glue. He dribbled between his legs and moved to his right. When he headed towards the basket, Shawn managed to jar the ball loose and knock it into the open court in the direction of his team's basket. With only six seconds left, he beat Roddy to the loose ball and headed towards his goal. Roddy was hot on his trail, but Shawn managed to shift into another gear as he glided to the basket and dunked the ball with authority as the clock ticked down to zero. He had pulled out the victory in the clutch.

Roddy stood at half court, with both hands on his head in disbelief. He was pissed and embarrassed. Not only did he get stripped, but Shawn's crowd pleasing dunk just poured more salt into his wounded ego. He stood with his hands on his hips and a distraught look on his face. His temper grew as the crowd went wild as they cheered on the winning team. They should've been cheering his team in victory, instead, it was the opposing team that received all of the accolades. To say Roddy was a sore loser was an understatement.

"Good game, man. You did your thing out there tonight," Shawn said as he tried to show good sportsmanship. He reached out to shake Roddy's hand as the two crossed each other at half court.

Roddy smacked his hand away. Shawn didn't seem fazed by his response. In fact, given their history, he expected Roddy to respond in such a childish manner as he did.

"Man, fuck you fool. That was a lucky play you got

off," Roddy spit back at him.

"Bro, that wasn't even necessary to slap my hand like that, but it's all good. You've always been a sore loser," Shawn uttered.

That was the wrong move on his part. He had just lit the fuse to a ticking time bomb. His words cut through Roddy like a freshly sharpened blade through flesh. Sensing that Roddy was about to explode, Sherman attempted to pull him in the opposite direction away from Shawn, but Roddy wasn't having that at all. He was too turned up to calm down.

"I'm a sore loser? I got your sore loser, bitch. Wait right here," Roddy barked as he stormed away.

Roddy walked over to the stands where his crew was seated. He reached into his black duffle bag that Petey had held for him and pulled out a snub nose .38 Revolver. He gripped it tightly and concealed it in the palm of his hand. He walked back towards Shawn, who was headed out of the gym to celebrate with his team. He had thought nothing more of his encounter with Roddy, because they had so many of them through the years, that he figured this would just be another verbal sparring, and they would go their separate ways. However, tonight was different. Roddy was on some other shit. He approached Shawn with his gat in tow and tapped him on the shoulder from behind.

"You still wanna run your mouth, bitch? You called me a sore loser? Is that what you said?" Roddy asked angrily.

"Roddy, chill man, I don't want no problems with you. It was a good game, and the best man won. Let's leave it at that, bro," Shawn said nonchalantly. He threw his hands in the air as if to say he submitted and didn't want any problems.

"Nah, don't back down now, partna. You were

feeling yourself a few minutes ago. Well feel these hot ones up in ya ass, bitch!" Roddy yelled.

Roddy pulled the trigger and let off three rounds into Shawn's chest. He fell to the floor, instantly covered in a pool of blood. He let off three more rounds in the air. The crowd scattered with everyone in a state of frenzy. It was sheer pandemonium. Everybody tried to make their way out of the building, looking for the nearest exit. There was so much commotion, that no one saw who actually did the shooting, with the exception of the few players that were standing next to Shawn. Roddy jetted out of the gym with his crew to make his escape while Shawn bled to death on the basketball court. They got lost in the crowd as they made their way to their cars in the parking lot.

"Man, what the fuck were you thinking about?" Sherman asked him angrily. He whipped the Lexus truck through the parking lot and onto the street. Petey and Dutch rode in the back seat.

"Yo, I wasn't thinking. I got caught up in the moment. That fool shoulda kept his mouth closed talking shit to me. He might still be alive right now," Roddy stated defiantly.

"Dog, are you for real? You know everybody saw you blast that fool, right? You think nobody is gonna give the police your description? It will only take a minute before the cops put two and two together and find your ass. Man, you just made the whole crew hot over a fucking basketball game, fam!" Sherman stated with contempt in his tone.

Clearly, Roddy didn't grasp the severity of his actions. He had always been known as a hot head that was quick to draw his gun out on a fool, when confronted. That ride or die mentality worked well in the trenches when you were engaged in battle in the streets, but when it came to verbal altercations with civilians, he lacked the personal restraint to deal with those situations diplomatically. Instead of letting something petty, such as a fool talking slick out of his mouth just ride, Roddy was the type of dude that had to have the last word or his gun would go off. It was just the way he was wired, plain and simple.

"Sherman, I ain't trying to hear that bull you talking. If a nigga run his mouth to me talking shit, then I'ma do'em, point blank, and I don't care who the fuck is around," Roddy chattered on. He was true to his word at all times. No one could fault him for his honesty. Right or wrong, anybody that knew Roddy knew how he got down. This incident was no surprise to those individuals. It was just business as usual for him.

By the time the paramedics and police arrived, Shawn had already crossed over to the other side. All that was left of him was a hollow physical shell for the coroner to examine and his family to bury. Because of Roddy's hot headedness, another local basketball legend had just died senselessly as a victim of Baltimore's inner city violence. A promising star would never reach his full potential, all because of a clash of egos on a basketball court. Once the dust settled, this incident would surely be all over the local and national news, given Shawn's status. The Money Kings crew would be the focus of the Baltimore City Police Department's attention for sure. The one thing that brings guaranteed heat from the law was an open murder case. JR would not be happy about the attention and spotlight this incident would shine on him and his organization. Killing a man over a basketball game in front of hundreds of witness was the dumbest move he could have made. Roddy would have to answer for this fuck up in a major way.

20

This is Jane Emerson, bringing you the news tonight for WBFF Fox 45. Well, the highlight of today's newscast is the mysterious deaths of several local college students from an accidental overdose from what has been described as a highly potent and lethal form of the new drug simply referred to as Molly. It appears that the highly addictive drug that is commonly found in nightclubs and rave parties has made its way from the rural sections of the West Coast to the suburban communities of Baltimore City and its surrounding counties. The Baltimore City Police Department reports that there has been an influx of these "party pills" over the last year in the city, and that they are working feverishly to uncover the identities of the major distributors of the drug.

While Ecstasy has been around for years, and authorities are well aware of its effects on the user, what separates Mollys from it as a hallucinogenic is that Ecstasy is MDMA mixed with other substances like cocaine. while Mollys are supposed to be pure MDMA not diluted with anything. This is supposed to create a more intense high and feeling of euphoria for the user. What stands out with the recently reported deaths of four college students is that all four seemed to have ingested Molly pills that were spiked with a lethal dosage of oxycodone. Medical experts report the oxycodone levels that were found in these pills were so potent, that it would kill a horse. The police are continuing their investigation of these deaths, which all appear to be connected to the same batch of bad drugs. This is a developing story and we will keep you posted as more details emerge.

In other news tonight, the scene at Webster M. Kendrick Recreation center in West Baltimore after a pickup game of basketball could best be described as pure chaos. Witnesses describe an act of cold blooded murder as University of Maryland basketball star and Baltimore native, Shawn Dandridge, was shot and killed after a dispute with a member of a notorious drug crew that known as the Money Kings. The police say that the notorious gang is the largest and most organized drug organization in the city, and is responsible for flooding the streets of Baltimore with large quantities of heroin and cocaine. The gang is led by a man named Nigel Hawkins, Jr., who has a history of drug related arrests. Witnesses report that Dandridge and his team had just played a game of basketball against the alleged gunmen's team when the verbal altercation broke out. Not soon afterwards, shots were fired and the gymnasium turned into another tragic murder scene.

Police have identified the gunman as twenty-year-old Roderick "Roddy" Winston, Jr. The police report that Mr. Winston has a rap sheet that includes charges such as attempted murder, second-degree assault, possession with intent to distribute cocaine, and armed robbery. He is also currently on probation for a handgun charge. He is reportedly a low-level street enforcer for the Money Kings, and considered to be armed and dangerous. Anyone having information that could lead to the arrest of Roddy Winston is asked to call the hotline number that is being flashed across the bottom of the screen. What makes this murder such a travesty, is that Shawn Dandridge, a young, intelligent, and super talented athlete will never go forward and fulfill his potential in the NBA. Sportscaster, Scott Barker will have more information on the impact that this local sports figure's death has had on the city, later on in the broadcast in the sports segment as he talks with his schoolmates and his college and high school basketball coaches as they mourn his tragic death.

JR wanted to crack the screen on his Samsung Galaxy Note tablet after viewing the video on the Fox News website. G Money saw the story earlier in the day and called JR to give him a heads up. Once he saw it for himself, his blood pressure began to boil.

"Fuck! Every time I turn around it's some new bullshit to deal with," JR ranted angrily.

"Son, what's the problem?" Nigel asked, sounding genuinely concerned. In reality, he was fishing for new information to feed to the Feds. The two had got together to take the boys out to play football in the park. They sat on the park bench and talked while the boys had a good time as they tossed the football around to each other.

"Pops, I swear being a boss in this game has its good days and bad days. This is gonna be one of those days that I got a feeling won't be considered a good one for some sad fool," he replied.

"What happened?" Nigel inquired further.

Before he could respond, JR was hit upside the head with the football. Quentin had thrown an errant pass to Malachi that somehow strayed in his direction. JR rubbed his temple to soothe the sting of the blow. He got up from his seat to retrieve the ball and threw it back over to the boys. They went back to playing their game of catch.

He was at his wits end, trying to figure out what went wrong with the last shipment of pills that he had distributed onto the streets of Baltimore. Somebody had obviously tampered with his product, and he needed to figure out how this occurred. Whoever was responsible for this foul up would be executed on sight, no questions asked. He had to send a clear message that this type of situation should never happen again.

The bad shipment of pills had to be manufactured at his facility in Philadelphia, because that was the closest one to the Baltimore area. G Money was responsible for overseeing the activities of the local Philly workers that they hired to run the Philadelphia facility. This foul up happened on his watch, and it would be his job to fix. It was time for him to earn his keep and show JR why he made him his top underboss.

As for Roddy, he couldn't believe that he could be so stupid as to kill somebody in front of a crowd of witnesses. On top of that, he killed somebody that was loved by the community and a national celebrity. This was the kind of press that JR did not need for his organization. As far as he knew, the Feds or the police had no evidence on him to build a case so far, but an incident like this one would certainly give them motivation to open a full-scale investigation into all of his illegal operations. The media lived for incidents like this. He was sure that they would be camped outside of the Money Kings Lounge, looking for him to make some form of statement. JR would definitely have to keep a low profile for a minute until the smoke cleared. As for Roddy, his fate was already sealed.

After the shooting went down, Roddy reached out to Demon to help get him out of the mess he had created. Demon, of course, hit JR up instantly and ran everything down to him. JR instructed Demon to stash Roddy at one of the apartments that they had situated around the city for emergency situations like this until he decided what he wanted to do with this trigger happy idiot. They had three such secret locations situated in obscure rural sections of the county areas where they were sure the police would be least likely to search for them if they ever needed to go on the lam. JR made sure that they were set up in a fake name and that the rent was paid on time to the landlord to avoid drawing any attention to them. Occasionally, at least once or twice a month either he or Demon would stay at each of the apartments for a few days so their neighbors would never get suspicious with not seeing anyone come and go from the apartments.

JR was sure that the police would be on his ass, applying pressure in an effort to locate Roddy. This situation had three solutions as far as he could see. Option one was that Roddy could turn himself in and face life in prison for the murder charge. If he did, JR would make sure that his family was taken care of as long as he kept his mouth closed. Option two was that he could stay on the run and try to make it out of the country to start a new life. He would be a fugitive for the rest of his years and would always have to look over his shoulder. This didn't seem like a good option because Roddy was dumber than a bag of hammers. JR didn't see him lasting too long before he made some stupid mistake to get himself captured. Once that went down, there was no guarantee that he wouldn't snitch to save himself. The third option that JR had was to have Demon execute him quickly and dispose of his body. That way, with no evidence of his death, it would appear that he had escaped. It would be the police's job to figure out that they were chasing after a dead man.

While they hunted for their man, JR could just sit back and let time do its thing in quelling their efforts to locate him. With no direct evidence to connect him to Roddy's disappearance, he would be in the clear. After mulling over the options overnight, JR made up his mind. He chose option number three. He had called Demon earlier that morning and gave him the green light. By now, he was sure that Roddy was somewhere chopped up into little pieces, floating in the bottom of the Chesapeake Bay. He was one less problem for him to worry about.

Truth be told, JR was no longer on his A game like he was just a year ago. Since he started popping Mollys on a regular basis, he had become addicted. One of the side effects of the drug was unpredictable mood swings. He also suffered from irrational thoughts and appeared to be distracted at times when he needed to be on point. He thought that since he started the money train rolling and put key people in place to run things for him, that he could sit back on autopilot and let his business run itself, but he was dead wrong. A boss always had to stay on point to make sure business got handled like it was supposed to be done.

"Well, did you see the story on the news last night about those college kids that overdosed on those Molly pills?" JR asked.

"Yeah, I watch the news every night. What does that have to do with you?" Nigel asked in response. The microphone wired to his chest was on to record their every word. He hoped that JR would give him something deemed useful by the agents who were stationed a distance away fully tuned in to their conversation.

"That was my product that they died from using.

Their deaths come back on me," JR responded. He sounded highly frustrated. He felt that he could confide in Nigel about his illegal dealings because he was his father. He trusted that their conversation would stay between them. If only he knew how wrong he was.

"JR, when did you get into selling pills? That's for white boys, I thought. I'm confused," Nigel stated.

He had known that his son sold cocaine and heroin, but he never envisioned him selling pills. He never imagined that they would be on his radar. Nonetheless, he prodded him for more good intel that the Feds could use in their case. He hoped this would all be over soon. It was eating at his soul that he had to betray his son in exchange for his freedom. He wanted to warn him that the Feds were on to him, but that would void his deal. It was a dog eat dog world out here, and he planned to be the pit bull that came out victorious in this battle. He gave enough of his life to the courts, jails, and streets. He did all he could to get JR to leave the streets alone, but he resisted him at every turn. Now it was time for him to live his life for him and his family. JR was a grown man, accountable for his own actions and would have to fend for himself.

"What are you confused about? If it makes dollars, it makes sense to me. Do you remember my plug that I told you about from up North, the Colombian dude?" JR asked.

"The guy named Julio?" Nigel asked in response. He made sure to invoke Julio's name in their conversation anytime he could, since he was the man that the Feds wanted and they made it clear they needed a direct connection between him and JR to make their case stick.

"Yup, he's one and the same. Well, he has that pill

market on lockdown across the country. He made me his point man over all of the East coast distribution market. It was an offer I couldn't refuse. It was too much money on the table to say no to. Now, after this, I'm starting to regret getting involved. Seeing a few deaths from a coke or dope overdose was one thing because the police expect that to happen. But with Mollys being the new hot drug on the streets, when somebody dies, the media is all over it like stank on shit. I don't need this type of heat in my life. I need to go see my lawyer now, so I can be prepared just in case them jump out boys come for me with questions. I ain't trying to see the inside of no cell over this bullshit. Let me get my driver to come pick me up," JR replied. He had rode to the park with Nigel in his car.

"Well, I can take the boys home if you need me to do so. That's not a problem at all. Go take care of your business," Nigel said sounding sincere.

"Thanks, Pops. I appreciate you man," JR said.

He pulled out his iPhone and sent Allen a text message to come pick him up. He had given him the keys to the Phantom earlier in the day to get it cleaned up at the detail shop. He motioned for the boys to come over to where he and Nigel were seated. He wanted to say goodbye to them before he bounced.

"What's up, daddy?" Quentin asked enthusiastically. He carried the football in his hands like a running back. He charged towards JR, who acted like a linebacker and grabbed him in a bear hold.

"Daddy has to make a run right quick. Pop Pop is gonna take you out to get whatever you want from the mall and then to Rita's to get an Italian ice," he replied.

"Daddy, you never have time for us lately," Savion chimed in. He wore a sad dejected look on his face.

"Yeah, Daddy, what's up with that?" Quentin interjected.

JR knew he wasn't on his job lately as a father. Once all of this drama was over, he planned to spend more time with them. He pulled them both to the side and sat them down on the bench next to them. Malachi took the football from Quentin and proceeded to play a game of catch with Nigel while JR and his boys talked father to sons.

"I know I've been busy lately, fellas, but just know that I love you two chumps and your mother more than anything else in this world. When I'm not around, just know that I'm working hard to make sure that we stay in that big house we live in and get to ride around in these fancy cars. Once I finish up this project I'm working on, the four of us are going on a nice vacation to wherever you guys wanna go," JR promised them.

"Ok, I guess we can let you slide this time. But don't make it a habit," Quentin said playfully.

"I love you, Daddy," Savion said as he hugged JR.

"I love you too, son," JR replied.

When JR turned around, he saw Allen pulling up in his car. The Phantom was sparkling clean with a shine so bright, it was blinding to the human eye. Everybody in the park turned around to marvel at its beauty. They wondered who the person was that owned this house on wheels. He had to be somebody important, they figured.

When Allen stepped out of the car to open the door for JR, Nigel's eyes opened wide in a state of shock. Allen looked in his direction as well.

"How's it going Mr. Hawkins? I haven't seen you in quite a while, sir," Allen stated respectfully.

"Yes, it has been a while since I last saw you, young man. What's your name again?" he asked in response.

"It's Allen, Mr. Hawkins," he replied.

"I'll have to remember that for the next time. Please forgive an old man. When you get my age, you get to be forgetful sometimes," Nigel joked. He was hardly in a joking mood.

Nigel just realized where he had seen the familiar face he ran across at the DEA office before. Allen was the man he saw seated in the interrogation room with the other agents. At that moment, it clicked in his head that the Feds already had a man on the inside of JR's organization feeding them intel. If Allen was JR's driver, he could only imagine how many incriminating conversations he overheard JR engaged in since he hired him. Nigel wanted to tip JR off, but he knew he couldn't because he would expose himself. It came full circle to Nigel that the Feds were pulling out all of the steps to seal the net around his son from all angles. With or without him cooperating, JR was going down.

JR and Nigel embraced each other before he got in the car. He gripped him extra tight and didn't want to let him go. When JR got in the car, Allen closed the door behind him. He and Nigel's eyes met as they were face to face. Allen nodded his head and shot Nigel an evil stare as if to say he knew his cover was blown, but Nigel better keep his mouth shut if he knew what was good for him.

Nigel turned and walked away from the car as they pulled off. He watched the boys continue to play and have a good time. He started to develop a migraine headache. He couldn't believe that after all that he had done to clean up his life, he could find himself in a jam like this one. He couldn't figure out a sensible way to get out of it without being harmed permanently in one way or another. He was caught between a rock and a hard place. His way out was really no way out, because it had horrible consequences. His life sucked and there wasn't a damn thing he could do about it, but suck it up and continue to go along with the plan. He was in too deep to turn back now.

21

JR had just left a good meeting with his attorney, Marlon Rhodes, and appeared to be in a good mood. His attorney assured him that he had nothing to worry about as of yet, with respect to being called in for questioning about the Shawn Dandridge murder or the recent overdose deaths. Mr. Rhodes had reached out to some of his higher up friends in the police department, and he was informed that there was no corroborating evidence to tie JR to either crime. At this point, any questions that came up, he told JR that he would handle them on his behalf. JR felt relieved to hear that news. It felt like a burden had been lifted off his shoulders. Now he could breathe again.

Marlon Rhodes was the best defense attorney in the state of Maryland. He graduated at the top of his class from Harvard University, and had a built a reputation for himself as a bulldog in the courtroom with the way he broke down prosecution cases and witnesses on the stand. He was well connected with all of the top judges in the city, so he was able to get things done that other attorneys in the city couldn't. He also had his hands in numerous shady business dealings with well-known underworld figures across the city. He was what one would describe as a gangster's attorney, because of ability to tow the line between that which was legal and criminal. That was also why JR paid him big money to keep him and his team out of jail. His intel was rarely off base, so JR felt confident that he was in the clear.

After they wrapped up their meeting, he decided to stop by to see Roshonda for minute. Some good dome from her would go a long way to helping him relax even more.

"Yo, Allen, swing me downtown for a minute so I can go see my African princess for a quickie," JR ordered.

"Sure thing, Boss," Allen replied. He had a big grin on his face.

"Why are you smiling like that, lil' homey?" JR asked.

"Oh, it's no particular reason, JR. You're just the man, and I wanna be just like you. You got all of this money, any woman that you want, and everybody respects you out in the streets," Allen replied gassing his already inflated ego.

"It took a lotta work for me to get here, lil' homey, but this life ain't for you. I see something bigger than what I'm doing in your future. How is school coming along?" JR asked.

"It's coming along great. I'm still getting all A's in my classes. I have about two more years before I get my degree," Allen replied.

"Getting a college degree and being able to talk all that fancy talk with them white folks, that's some boss shit too, lil' fella. Shit, you'll be making six figures and more in no time as smart as you are. One bit of advice that you better always remember that I told you, is don't ever sell yourself short. This thug thing is something I was born into and I can't shake it no matter how hard I try, but you got a chance to do something different. I don't want this life for my sons. That's why I send them to private schools to get the best education that this country has to offer. I want them to be like you," JR spoke sincerely.

"I don't know what to say, but thanks, JR. Your support means the world to me," Allen lied.

Allen was consumed with mixed emotions about JR. On the one hand, given that he was a federal agent working undercover, he knew that it was his job to bring JR to justice for his numerous criminal activities. On the other hand, this man showed him nothing but love and support for his fictitious life as a struggling college student. He dissuaded him away from a life of crime and encouraged him to make a better legal life for himself. He couldn't understand how someone could be so ruthless in taking lives and selling drugs like JR did, but at the same time, be a good dude in his heart. He wished that they could have met under different circumstances, because he could see them genuinely being friends. Allen regretted that he had to betray JR's trust, but he knew he had a job to do. JR was a primary subject in a federal investigation, and he was the undercover agent sent in to bring him down.

"What the fuck?" JR yelled.

When Allen was about to pull out of the parking lot, a black sedan pulled up right behind them to block their path from leaving. Two burly, Colombian men got out of the car and walked towards the Phantom on each side. JR reached for his gun that was stored in the secret compartment in the back seat that he had installed when he bought the car. Before he could get it out of the compartment, the two men opened the rear car doors and got inside with JR, surrounding him on both sides.

"It would be in your best interest to put that gun away. Our good friend wants to see you, now," one of the men spoke firmly.

Allen observed the whole scene, paying close attention to every movement of the two men that had accosted his boss. He was surprised at how their peaceful day had changed into a dramatic one so quickly. In the streets, things could get real like that in the blink of eye. Nonetheless, Allen remained calm and waited patiently to see how things played out.

JR felt at ease. These were Julio's people. They were family. He had no reason to fear these two muscular goons. He pushed the gun back into the compartment and closed the door. The two men got out of the car and JR followed behind them en route to the sedan. One of the goons got in the front seat, while the other one got in the back along with JR.

"Damn, Julio. What the hell are you doing in Baltimore?" JR asked.

"JR, my friend, I must say I am extremely disappointed in you. I gave you the keys to paradise and you fucked it up," Julio said in a calm calculated tone. He took a deep pull off his Cuban cigar and exhaled.

"What the hell are you talking about, Julio? We are making money hand over fist out here for you. What more do you want?" JR asked.

"Do you remember when I told you that if you follow my advice, then you will be successful in your new role? Do you remember when I said to stay low key and keep your nose clean?" he asked.

"Yeah, and I have done just that, so I don't see what the problem is," JR shot back.

"Then tell me why the hell do I see on the front page of the news that one of your fucking little goons murdered a big time basketball player in front of a gang of witnesses? How stupid was that? Why do I have to get information coming back to me that one of my manufacturing plants has been tampered with and caused four white kids to die? I left you in charge of the whole East Coast operation and you fucked it up," Julio said angrily.

"Hold up, Julio, let me say something. I'm on top of everything. That guy that killed the basketball player, he's history, done, never to be heard from again. As for the fuck up at the plant, I got my people..." JR spoke before Julio cut him off.

"Don't waste your time. I have already had my people go in and clean that shit up. But that's not all. It's seems that your team is not as solid as it appears to be. You have a rat in your house that needs to be put to sleep," Julio said with clear intent and purpose.

"Now, Julio, I know I made mistakes, but all of my crew is soldiers. Ain't no rat on my team. I vetted everybody myself personally," JR said with confidence.

"Are you sure about that? Well how do you explain this?" Julio asked. He shoved a slew of pictures at JR.

JR's whole mood changed. He shifted in his seat. He wore a look on his face like his whole world had just crumbled. The insight on his legal situation that he just got from Martin couldn't have been more wrong. Clearly, Julio had more pull than him in the legal system and access to more information than Martin did. The pictures that Julio showed him were of Nigel meeting with agents Parks and Anderson at various locations. There was nothing he could say. He didn't want to believe his own eyes, but facts were facts. Nigel Hawkins, his father, the OG that taught him all he knew, had sold him out and now played for the other team. He was crushed.

"Where did you get these photos from?" JR asked, still in disbelief.

"I told you, I have friends in high places that you

could never imagine. I know and see everything. You are so smart, and such a fucking boss, but you didn't even see that your own father was a mole right in front of your eyes. The Feds have been building a case against you for quite some time. They wanna use you to get to me. It got me to thinking that maybe you might be a snitch too," Julio stated maliciously.

"Julio, I ain't no rat. I'm about this life to the death of me. I put that on everything that I love," JR stated in an attempt to defend his gangster.

"I hear your words, JR, but if you want to prove to me that you are not a rat, you know what you have to do. You clean up this mess and I'll consider using my influence to get you outta this. As it stands, I hold the keys to your life or your death, my friend. The choice is yours," Julio stated with resolute conviction.

"It's a done deal," JR stated bluntly. He was filled with so much rage at Nigel for selling him out that he wanted his head on platter, served up for carving.

"You've got forty-eight hours to make it happen, my friend. After that time expires, all bets are off," Julio stated.

Julio gave JR the look of death to ensure that his message was clear. It was either his life or Nigel's. JR knew that he had to what he had to do to save his own life and the lives of his family. He had been in this situation before, dealing with Polo. However, this time was different. His father got a pass back then. This time around, there would be no compromise. His judgment day had arrived. A rat had to be dealt with accordingly; even it was his own flesh and blood.

JR got out of the car and walked back over to the Phantom slowly, as if the life had been sucked out of him. He wondered what the Feds had on his father to make him flip on him. He thought about all of the recent conversations he had with his father about his business dealings, and realized how fucked he was if the Feds got their hands on any of the damaging statements that he had made to Nigel about himself and Julio. It all became clear to him why Nigel appeared to be so concerned about his business dealings lately. It wasn't out of love and concern for him, but it was to get him to talk openly about his illegal dealings. He used his trust against him. This was the ultimate betrayal in his eyes. Nigel would have done better to just drive a knife through JR's heart than to rat on him. His retribution for being betrayed would surely be something sinister.

"Boss, who was that? Is everything okay?" Allen asked when he got back in the car.

"Don't ask me no fucking questions, man. Just drive the fucking car! Just drive, got dammit!" JR demanded.

Allen pulled the car out of the parking spot, and did as he was instructed. He figured that the Colombian men had to have some connection to Julio, and that the meeting had to be about something heavy. He had no idea that Nigel's cover was blown. The mood that JR was in told him to not ask any more questions of JR, or he might feel his wrath. Allen planned to report the unscheduled meeting to his superiors the first chance that he got. Whoever was in the car that JR got into was someone high up in the Gomez cartel food chain. He had no clue that it was Julio himself.

JR sat in the back with vengeance on his mind. Heaven help Nigel, because what JR had planned for him was some real ungodly shit.

22

Agent Anderson sat behind his desk and sipped on a strong cup of Black coffee. His reading glasses hung down on his nose. He hacked heavily, with a consistent cough that he had developed over the years from smoking so many cigarettes and cigars. He walked with a slight lean, due to having a herniated disc removed from his back a few years ago. Anderson leaned his chair back against the wall and put his feet up on his desk as he reviewed his notes that detailed the long list of evidence that he had against JR and Julio. The deck was stacked so high against these two villains, that in his mind, there was no way they could lose this case. It was an open and shut slam-dunk of an investigation, that he was damn proud to be one of the lead agents on. He just sat back and imagined how it would feel to be in his new administrative office after this case was wrapped up.

While Anderson was busy with his fantasies of career advancement, Agent Parks was in the lobby becoming frustrated waiting for Nigel to arrive. Today, they planned to do their final debriefing of him before they went to the Attorney General's office to seek indictments in the case. He was supposed to arrive at five o'clock, but he was already forty-five minutes late for their appointment. This was unlike him as he was always on time to meet them whenever they requested his presence, either at the office, or at a clandestine location. Parks started to feel worried that Nigel might have gotten cold feet and did something stupid to jeopardize their case. He hoped that he didn't let his guilty conscious lead him to warn JR about his impending indictment, because if he did, they planned to use the full arm of the law to make his life a living hell in every imaginable manner.

Jail would've been an easy way out for Nigel once they finished destroying his life and the lives of everyone that he loved, if he backed out of their deal. His anxiety was laid to rest when he saw Nigel walk towards the front with Nicole and Albert by his side. They had left Malachi with Mama Hawkins while they handled this business. She had no clue what they were about to do. If she did, she would have put a stop to everything. She would never cosign Nigel betraying JR like this in any situation. That was why he kept her in the dark, and planned to do so until the very last minute before he was whisked away into federal custody. Parks looked at his watch and let out a huge sigh as they walked towards him.

"Sorry to keep you waiting. There was a bad accident on the beltway and we were stuck in traffic. I apologize for the inconvenience of your time," Albert stated politely.

If Albert wanted sympathy or empathy, there was none to be found with Parks. He was clearly focused on what Nigel could do for them and their case and nothing else. His personal issues were just that... his to deal with in his own way and on his own time. He was a cooperating witness in a federal investigation and had a job to do. Nothing else mattered.

"Right this way. Have a seat in the room to the left. My partner and I will be with you shortly," Parks instructed them.

As they walked towards the room, Nigel shot him an evil glare to express his contempt with the whole situation. Parks left them to talk amongst themselves while he went to get Anderson.

Nigel had visibly aged quite a bit in his appearance from the toll the investigation took on his mind and body. He didn't sleep much and ate just enough to keep from starving. Nicole, on the other hand, had a more of a positive disposition about the entire ordeal. She was relieved that once this all over, JR would finally be out of their lives for good. She would have her husband and son to all to herself. Even if they had to give up their business and beautiful home in the process to go into witness protection it would all be worth it in the end for them to be together living in peace. She would finally have the family that she always dreamed of having. She reasoned that Nigel's mixed feelings would fade away over time as he adjusted to his new life.

"Baby, this will all be over soon, and we can put this chapter behind us," Nicole reasoned.

"Honey, please don't talk right now. I don't wanna argue with you. I just wanna get this over with as soon as possible. I don't know if I'll ever be able to put selling out my son behind me," Nigel said sternly.

"Yes, let's just get through this and deal with the rest later," Albert interjected in an attempt to keep the peace. He saw that the two of them were on the edge of a combustible explosion.

Moments later, Parks and Anderson entered the room. They both walked with a confident stride. They held all the cards in the deck and they knew that this case theirs to blow.

"Hawkins, I gotta, as you black folks say, 'keep it real' with you. I didn't think you could pull this thing off for us. We've been trying to get JR to talk about his business operation for the past two years, but came up empty. In a matter of months, you have him spilling his guts to you about everything. I guess that father and son bond is good for something, huh?" Agent Parks joked.

Nigel sat stoned faced and emotionless as Parks made his silly taunts and jabs. He tried his best to remain calm. He hadn't felt this kind of rage inside since he killed Polo years ago. His brutal temper was something that he was proud to have managed to tame over the years. However, right now, he felt like he was about to lose control.

"Come on, Parks, let's not rub it in too bad. Nigel is our friend, aren't you buddy?" Anderson joked adding insult to injury.

Parks laughed so hard that he almost fell out of his chair. Frustrated that he had to involve himself in the legal lynching they had planned for his son, Nigel couldn't take their taunts any longer. He lunged at him across the table and wrapped his hands around Parks' neck.

"You think you're funny, motherfucker? You think that this is a game? That's my son you're talking about! You think I'm proud of what I've done? I feel like shit!" Nigel screamed. His grip was so tight around Parks' neck that he lifted him out of his seat.

"Nigel... No! Please calm down! Don't do this baby!" Nicole pleaded. Her cries fell upon deaf ears.

"Hawkins, you better calm down and get ya grimy hands off my partner before I put two slugs in that nigga dome of yours," Anderson threatened. He had his 9 mm pointed directly at Nigel's temple and waited for a reason to pull the trigger.

"You think that gun scares me? Go ahead, pull the trigger! I'm already dead anyway. I've lost my son. I sold my soul to the devil! What else do I have to lose?"

Nigel rambled. He was clearly at his breaking point. The moral battle that he had waged with himself over snitching on JR had him not thinking clearly at all. When he told Anderson to pull the trigger, a part of him meant it seriously. Death would be an easy way out of the situation for him.

"Nigel, calm down, brother. Think about Malachi. You know your son needs his father. Get your hands off his neck! Please, brother, turn him loose," Albert pleaded with him.

Albert looked at Anderson and he hoped he would continue to exercise restraint and not pull the trigger. He didn't want Nigel to die. They had worked too hard to build a relationship, for him to lose him in this manner. It was bad enough he would have to go into witness protection. At least in that situation, he knew he would be alive. Nigel came back to his senses and loosened his grasp around Park's neck. Anderson put his gun away. Calm had been restored to the room.

"You crazy motherfucker, be lucky that we need you for this case, or I would take you out back and shoot you myself," Parks threatened. He used his hands to massage his sore neck that had turned red from the force of Nigel's grip. Anderson nudged him to get him back on track.

"Let's get this over with so we can be done with you, Hawkins. We have paperwork that we need for you to sign, indicating that no form of coercion was used to get your son to talk about his crimes, and that he did so of his free will. We also have the paperwork here for you to sign indicating the terms of your witness protection agreement.

"I'll take those forms. Please allow me a moment to look them over," Albert stated. The agents nodded their head in agreement. Albert reviewed the paperwork to insure that no detail of the agreed upon terms was left out of the deal.

As part of the agreement to testify and become an informant for the DEA, Albert managed to convince them to allow Nigel and Nicole to be able to liquidate some of their assets and accounts so that they would have a healthy financial nest egg, which they could use to build a new life. The Feds wanted JR and Julio bad enough that they agreed to this unusual condition. After short selling a few properties and liquidating several bank accounts, they were able to put together close to three quarters of a million dollars in cold hard cash. That was more than enough money to sustain them for quite some time. Albert reviewed the paper, and everything was written in the agreement as negotiated.

"Everything is in order, Nigel. I just need you to sign on the dotted line.

Nigel grabbed a pen off the table and signed all of the forms in the appropriate places. With his signature as the seal, the only thing left for him to do was to testify at JR's upcoming trial. Nicole grabbed his other hand to signify their solidarity. Tonight would be his last night of freedom before his life changed forever, because they would be secured away at a secret location beginning tomorrow until the trial was over.

With the recordings that Nigel was able to get of JR admitting to his business relationship with Julio, his boasting about his millions of dollars of unreported income that would surely be of interest to the IRS, and his statements about his involvement in the murders of Shep and his crew in East Baltimore, they had plenty. Albert was sure that there was more than enough damaging evidence to get indictments against JR and his Money Kings crew.

In addition to Nigel's recorded conversations,

they also had Allen's eyewitness testimony about the inner workings of JR's organization. He had witnessed numerous drug transactions involving Nigel and his top lieutenants and other major drug dealers across the city. He was present for the planning of numerous murders and retaliation shootings orchestrated by Demon and his slew of young goons. The noose was about to tighten around JR's neck soon, and he would unable to loosen its grasp. He was living on borrowed time for sure.

Parks and Anderson also had another surprise witness they planned to call as their ace in the hole. When Parks came up with the idea to leave the envelope filled with pictures of JR engaged in kinky sex with Roshonda and several other females on the windshield of Rochelle's car, they had calculated correctly that seeing first hand her husband's infidelity would push her over the edge and make her want revenge. They also cleverly planted a false sonogram picture in the package to suggest that Roshonda was pregnant by JR. Finally, the threat of losing custody of Quentin and Savion was the last straw that convinced her to cooperate and waive her spousal privilege to testify against JR.

They knew that no mother who loved her children as much as Rochelle did would choose her husband over them if her back was against the wall. Once JR looked up to see Rochelle's face on the witness stand to testify against him, they just hoped that he didn't keel over and die on the spot. They wanted him to spend the rest of his days on Earth suffering in a federal jail cell for all of the carnage and death he had caused in his life of crime.

Once all of the paperwork was signed, Nicole, Albert, and Nigel, hopped back into his car. Albert planned to drop them off at their home to spend one last evening together before their worlds were turned upside down. He was disappointed and hurt that his brother, who he had grown to love, would be gone soon, but he accepted it as a reality he would have to endure. Besides, he had to be strong for his mother once she found out the news. It would surely break her heart not to see Nigel again.

"What the hell are you doing fool? Turn those bright lights off!" Albert swore in an episode of road rage.

He swerved out of his lane when the high beam lights from the vehicle behind them shined bright enough to block his vision temporarily. He regained his focus long enough to look over his shoulder to see the speeding vehicle come up on his right side. The window on the van rolled down and before he had time to react, several shots were fired into the vehicle. Albert lost control of the car and it crashed into a tree. He died instantly from the gunshot wound to his neck and from the trauma of his head hitting against the windshield.

"This can't be real! Albert wake up! Wake up!" Nigel screamed at the corpse of his lifeless brother positioned in the driver's seat. His words fell upon deaf ears. He reached his hand around to touch his neck to feel for a pulse, but there was none. Albert had already crossed over to the other side.

Nigel was in the back seat of the car and somehow managed to miss being hit by the gunfire. The only injury he sustained was a gash on his head from hitting it on the passenger window. It might require several stitches, but he would live.

"Nigel. Call 911, baby! I don't think I'm gonna make it. I love you, baby. Tell Malachi that Mommy loves him with all of her heart," Nicole said in a very faint voice.

Nigel looked at her seated in the front passenger seat and saw that she was covered in blood on her neck and in her chest area. The blood gushed out like a river flowing. She had been hit by several bullets in the ambush. Nigel got out of the car and opened up the passenger door to get to her. He pulled her body out of the car and laid her in the grass.

"Hold on for me, baby. Just hold on! I'm calling 911 now!" Nigel screamed as he cradled her in his arms. He used his free hand to reach for his cell phone that was in his jacket pocket. When he retrieved it, he dialed 911 and the got the operator on the line.

"911, is this an emergency?" the operator asked.

"Yes, I need an ambulance. My wife and brother have been shot. We were run off the road by a black van. They just opened fire on our car. We swerved off the road and hit a tree. It was a hit. I think there are two men involved. Get a message to DEA agents Parks and Anderson and tell them that my son, JR Hawkins, has sent somebody to kill me. Please send an ambulance. My wife is bleeding to death!" Nigel pleaded.

Before he could hear the next words from the operator, a shadowy figure in a mask appeared in front of him and fired two more shots into Nicole. She stopped breathing instantly. Another man came up from behind Nigel and hit him over the head with the butt of his gun, knocking him unconscious. His phone fell to the ground, but the operator was still on the line.

"You worthless piece of shit!" one of the men said angrily.

"I got his arms. Get his feet," the other man said.

The operator overheard them as they continued to talk. The two men lifted Nigel's body off the ground and carried him up the hill. They tossed him in the back of the van. One of the men got in the back with him while the other one hopped in the driver's seat. The two assassins drove off the scene with Nigel in tow. He had just lost the love of his life and his brother. Death seemed like a peaceful escape from the tragedy that just transpired.

23

Less than an hour ago, Agents Parks and Anderson were in their zone. They had all of the key pieces in place for their investigation to be considered a smashing success. A gang of arrests and convictions would surely soon follow. They envisioned the lofty pay increases they would receive, in addition to their inevitable rise through the ranks. However, all of their hard work was now in jeopardy, and they were clueless as to how it had happened so fast. Somebody dropped the ball in a major way for them to be headed to the scene of a double murder. Anderson parked the squad car and the two agents walked down the hill to the murder scene.

"Fuck! Fuck! Fuck! How in the hell did this happen? This is a fucking catastrophe!" Agent Anderson screamed.

Luckily, the 911 operator was diligent in alerting the police right away. The police, in turn, got a message to the agents as Nigel had instructed. They sensed that this had something to do with a major case that they had in the works. When they arrived on the scene and saw the carnage that was left behind, the police wasted no time in placing a call to the DEA office. Parks and Anderson arrived in record time on the scene. None of them were prepared for what they saw.

Parks surveyed the scene of the brutal carnage that took place less than two miles away from the DEA office. Albert's car was wrapped around a tree and his dead carcass was slumped over the steering wheel. Nicole's body was found laid out on the ground, riddled with bullets and covered in blood. Nigel was nowhere to be found. This was the worst-case scenario for Parks and Anderson, because they had failed to provide adequate protection for their confidential informant. They should have never let Nigel leave their office after he signed his deal without ample protection. They would have to explain this whole mess to their superiors. They would be lucky if they kept their jobs after this foolish blunder.

"Somebody must have tipped JR off that his father was working with us. We have to have a mole in our office somewhere. That's the only way he could've known. Now they have Hawkins, and there's no telling where the hell they are," Anderson reasoned.

"Agents, I'm Detective Baker. I'm one of the lead homicide detectives on this case. We've put an all-points bulletin out for JR Hawkins, his accomplice, and his father, Nigel. We have the whole force scouring the city looking for these ruthless killers. They won't get far," the police detective stated confidently. He was one of the first officers on the scene and acted swiftly in implementing a plan of action to catch the killers.

"I hope you're right, JR Hawkins is one slippery bastard," Anderson stated.

"I am well aware of the history of Mr. Hawkins. I know JR very well. He and his drug gang are notorious throughout the city. His main muscle guy, Demon is a wicked son of a bitch. He kills for sport. I tried to pin several murders on his Money Kings crew through the years, but I could never make a case stick.

Either there were no witnesses, or if there was a witness, they were too scared to testify. Whenever I interviewed Demon, he was always cool, calm and collected when I showed him pictures of his victims. He would just smile and deny any involvement. He is the definition of a psychopath," Detective Baker stated honestly in a frustrated tone.

"One thing for sure is that they must surely be desperate for him to pull a move like this so close to our office. This had to be some spur of the moment planning, because this was a sloppy job on their part," Parks reasoned.

"You might be right, partner. You may have a good point there. We might just have a good chance to grab them both before they get in the wind. I wanna see both of those evil motherfuckers rot in a cell for the rest of their lives," Detective Baker stated enthusiastically.

"I've already dispatched a team to JR's home to get Rochelle before he has a chance to get to her next. There is no telling how much intel he has been privy to throughout this investigation. We need to keep them safe until we catch this bastard. If he tried to kill his father like this, you know damn well he would put a bullet in his wife's brain to save his own ass in a heartbeat," Anderson stated.

While the three men talked, the federal agents and city police, continued to collect evidence from the scene. The newscasters and press had arrived and were like vultures attempting to get statements from the detectives and pictures of the tragic murder scene. It all looked like something out of a Scorsese film with all of the drama and high anxiety that filled the area. However, not even Scorsese could have scripted a drama this treacherous and bestial in nature.

Time was not on JR's side right now. With the

police scouring the city in pursuit of him, and his face plastered all over the news, he had few places to go without being recognized by somebody. He was considered to be armed and dangerous. Police officers were instructed to be cautious when approaching him and to use deadly force to subdue him and Demon if necessary. A reward for his capture would surely be the next option that the DEA would pursue to bring him to justice. JR was a dead man walking.

24

JR paced frantically back and forth across the filthy piss stained carpet. The walls of the dilapidated house were covered with graffiti. Trash and debris were scattered throughout the place. The house reeked of alcohol and the smell of musky ass from all of the bums that squatted there from time to time. This filthy rat trap was not a place you would find a boss like JR, but it was the place that he used to call home when he was a child. Just being there brought back memories of the manic childhood he had, growing up the product of two drug-addicted parents. His mind raced with thoughts of the many arguments his father and mother used to have when the drugs got low. He remembered all of the men that used to share his mother's bed when his father was gone for days on a drug binge. His childhood was filled with many days and nights alone as he cried himself to sleep on an empty stomach.

JR remembered like it was yesterday, the day his father was sentenced to prison and he went to live with his grandmother. He thought about how crushed he was to have to grow up so many years without him in his life. It was the main reason that even though he forgave Nigel and let him back in his life, he still had a dark side to him that remained cold and heartless. That dark side of him was in plain view right now as he contemplated exactly how he planned to end the life of the man that gave him life. He loved Nigel immensely, because he was his father, but he hated him just as intensely for setting him up with the Feds. He was in a no man's land where he had to choose to give in to his dark side and send Nigel into a state of purgatory for his betrayal or he could show him mercy and spare his life. Either way, he knew he was going to jail.

While JR contemplated his next move, Nigel began to awaken from the brutal beating that he and Demon had inflicted on him since they abducted him from the murder scene. He had several broken ribs and internal bleeding for sure from all of the heavy blows he received. His face was filled with burn marks from the cigarette butts that Demon put out on it repeatedly. Demon broke both of his wrists so that he couldn't use his hands to defend himself. Nigel was helplessly at their mercy to do with him what they wished.

The last forty-eight hours for JR seemed more like a lifetime. So many things had changed for him in that short time span, which left him in an ever moving tailspin towards his own demise. He was on top of the world with all of the money, notoriety, and power that one young uneducated Black man from the hood could ask for, but it all seemed to dwindle away in the blink of an eye. The millions of dollars that he had at his disposal could do nothing to save him from spending the rest of his life in jail at the very least, considering all of the damaging statements he had made to his father that might have been recorded by the Feds. They would more than likely go for the death penalty for him and Demon both. He had nothing to lose at this point. And it was all due to Nigel giving them the information that they needed to bury him.

"You recognize this place, Pops?" JR asked Nigel as he lifted his head off the ground.

He opened his swollen eyelids as best he could to look around the room. He knew the layout of the home and it looked familiar. All of a sudden, it all came back to him.

"This is the same house that your mother and I used to live in when you were born," Nigel replied.

"Ding. Ding. Demon, he gets a reward for guessing the right answer," JR said with a grin full of chicanery.

"You got it, boss," Demon replied. He winked at JR and proceeded to physically abuse Nigel some more. Nigel winced in pain as Demon did what he did best... put the hurt on somebody with no remorse. Compassion was not a word that Demon would ever use to describe how he treated an enemy. He was a heartless monster, but he was a monster that was loyal to JR.

"So here we are, Pops. All of these years of the Hawkins men running wild in the streets has come down to this? From Granddaddy Augustus Hawkins passing down his street wisdom to you and you teaching me the game from the time I was in pampers, this is what it all boils down to, huh? All of those long conversations about loyalty, honor, and being a soldier in the streets, and is this how it all ends? I brought you here because I wanted your last memory to be of the place where all of the fucked up shit you taught me started. This is where you and that junkie bitch of a mother of mine fucked my life up totally," JR said. He was on an adrenaline high right now, and nothing could be done to bring him down.

"JR please let me explain, son. Please don't do this. I had no choice. The Feds had me with my back against the wall. They were gonna take my business away and send me back to jail if I didn't cooperate. Nicole was pressuring me to make a decision to choose her and Malachi over you, and I panicked," Nigel tried to explain.

Before he could finish making a futile attempt to save his life, JR took his foot and drop kicked him in the chest. The blow knocked the wind out of him.

"Nicole? You wanna use that bitch as an excuse for what you did to me? She never really liked me anyway, but I still tried to deal with her on the strength of you. You're trying to tell me that you let her convince you to turn on me? Get the fuck outta here," JR said growing even more furious.

"You're right, son. I can't blame anybody else but me for what I did to you, but killing me is not gonna solve your problem. You're just as fucked up as me if you wanna be real about all of this. It's true that I turned you on to the streets, but I also did everything I could to get you out of them as well. How many times have I told you to take your money and get out of the drug game? How many times, JR?" Nigel reasoned as he spit out blood.

JR just laughed as he hovered over him.

"Nigga, please. Don't go pulling that bullshit with me. That reverse psychology can't help ya ass now. Don't ever try to speak to me in that fatherly tone. That shit has no effect on me. Yeah, you did try to get me out of the game that you got me into from the beginning. That part is true, but then you go and rat on me? I mean, Pops, why didn't you come to me? I got money and the best lawyers in the world. We coulda fought your case together. My guys woulda made an income tax evasion case go away in a heartbeat. Instead of being a soldier, you went out like a bitch and wanted to take me down with you," JR reasoned.

"You're right, son. I'm guilty as charged. I know this probably doesn't matter to you right now, but son, I love you. I love you with all of my heart. You're my first born. I remember when I brought you home from the hospital. I was proud at that moment. I swore to do everything I could to give you a good life. I failed in that promise. I know I did, miserably. But son, you wouldn't kill your own father would you? Think about how that would hurt your grandmother," Nigel said in a desperate attempt to appeal to JR's cold heart. Mama Hawkins was the one person that JR cherished in the world more than anything.

JR laughed at this statement. He looked at Demon with a smirk on his face.

"Oh, no this motherfucker didn't just use my grandmother's name to try and save his own ass. Man, you are unbelievable. You are not the man I thought you were. We are not one in the same. You're right, I can't kill you myself. Demon, it's time to feast, my friend," JR said abruptly. He raised his hand and ran it along his neck in a cutting motion. It was sign that Demon knew too well.

"JR, I'm not the only one you have to worry about betraying you. You have another rat in your camp. Al—" Nigel stated before he was cut off in midsentence.

Before he could get Allen's name out of his mouth to let him know that he was a federal agent, Demon had slit his throat. Blood gushed out everywhere as he bled to death. Nigel Hawkins, the man, the legend, was no more. JR couldn't look at him because it cut too deep into his soul. His love/hate relationship with his father was now officially over.

"JR, we gotta get the hell up outta here now. It won't be too long before the Feds catch up with us if we stay around much longer. We need to torch this place," Demon stated, breaking him out of his trance.

"You're right, Demon. Go get the gasoline," JR ordered.

Demon went to retrieve the gas can from the front area of the house. When he came back into the room where Nigel's body was, he was greeted by JR's gun pointed at his head. He couldn't believe what he saw. JR planned to kill him as well. After all of his loyalty, and all of the bodies he caught for him, it didn't matter to him at all.

"JR, what the fuck, man? We're supposed to be like brothers, dawg. You're gonna do me like this?" Demon asked, copping a plea.

"Sorry, my friend, but this is the way it has to be. It's nothing personal. I gotta look out for me. We'll see each other again... in hell," JR stated coldly as he pulled the trigger three times.

All three shots hit Demon in the head. His massive frame lay lifeless next to Nigel. JR grabbed the gas can and doused both bodies in gasoline. He poured the rest of the gas on the carpet throughout the place as he made his way to the front door. He lit a match and watched as the flames spread throughout the house. The fire igniting, symbolized the end of the last remnant of his past. He shut the door behind him and ran to the van. He pulled off and continued with his plan to try and avoid capture.

JR needed to get out of town quick, fast, and in a hurry, but he wasn't leaving without Rochelle and his boys. They were all he had left in the world. He would miss his grandmother dearly, but he didn't have time to say goodbye to her. He planned to ditch the van and have Allen pick him up at a remote location so that he could try to get out of the state and catch a flight out of town from Virginia. However, first, he had to hit up one of houses where he stashed his emergency cash for situations like this one. The particular house that he had in mind to hit up had over a million dollars secured away in a safe. That would be more than enough money for him and his family to start a new life in a foreign country. He placed a call to Rochelle to tell her where to meet him with the boys, but she didn't answer. JR was in a race against time and the deck was stacked against him, but he was determined to find a way out of this mess he created.

"Hello, who is this?" Allen asked half asleep.

"It's me, JR. Yo, I need you to pick me up downtown at the Inner Harbor by Scully's restaurant in like an hour. Before you come get me though, I need you to go my house and get Rochelle and my kids for me. She's not answering her phone. I don't have anybody else to turn to right now, Allen. Things are hot for me. The Feds are on my ass and I gotta get outta town. Do me this last solid, and there's a hundred grand in it for you," JR promised.

"I'm on it, boss. No worries. I got you," Allen stated. He hung up the phone with JR and placed a call to agent Anderson at the DEA office.

"This is agent Anderson here," he answered the phone.

"Anderson, this is Allen. I think I've got some good news that will make your day," he stated.

"What's that?" he asked.

"I just a got a call from JR Hawkins. He wants me to meet him downtown to help him and his family get outta town in an hour," Allen replied.

"Holy shit! That's damn good news. I'll round up a team now so we can catch this motherfucker! Allen, your future with the agency just got a helluva lot brighter," Anderson declared as he hung up. He wasted no time in rounding up a team to set up a trap for JR. They had him right where they wanted him.

They had bungled the case the last time, when they went after the DFL crew, by letting Dayvon get away, but this time was gonna be different. They would be damned if they let JR slip out of their grasp. He was going to be captured tonight, dead or alive.

25

Allen arrived at the location where he was to meet JR in exactly an hour alone. Rochelle and the kids weren't with him obviously, because they were in protective custody. He would have to make up a good lie to tell JR, for why they weren't with him. He knew if JR didn't see them in his car, he would instantly get suspicious and try to make an attempt to get away.

As he awaited JR's arrival, Allen placed a call. The person answered on the first ring.

"Hello, nephew, I hope you have some good news for me," Julio stated.

Julio Gomez was Allen's uncle. His mother, Emily, was Julio's illegitimate sister by a black woman named Isadora that their father, Javier, had fallen in love with many years ago when he was sent to the United States to attend college. When Julio's grandparents found out that Javier got Isadora pregnant, they paid her a lump sum of money to go away so that she wouldn't hinder his chances of finishing college. Isadora wound up connecting back up with Javier many years later and introduced him to his daughter, Emily. The two of them connected instantly in a strong father to daughter bond as though they were never separated.

Javier loved her just as much as he loved Julio and his other children. He brought her to Colombia to introduce her to the rest of her siblings. Julio's brothers initially gave Emily the cold shoulder because she was half black, but not Julio. He embraced his sister with open arms. When she became pregnant with Allen, he was a proud uncle and treated him like he was his own son.

Julio paid for Allen's college education and encouraged him to join the DEA and become an agent. In exchange for his help with college, Allen provided inside information to his uncle about any investigations that might involve him. That was how Julio always managed to stay a step ahead of the authorities all of the time. Allen was solid agent, and had broken numerous big cases for the agency. He was also equally solid at being an inside man for his uncle and any of his associates that were willing to pay a hefty fee for valuable tips on any possible legal situations. He played both sides of the fence well.

"Let's just say that your JR problem is about to go away," Allen stated.

"Ahhh, that's good news. Keep me posted, nephew," Julio replied.

"Will do," Allen said. He was startled by a knock on the driver's side window. It was JR and he didn't look happy. He rolled down the window to the car.

"Where the fuck is my family?" JR asked.

Before Allen could respond, federal agents swooped down out of nowhere and surrounded JR. All of their guns were drawn. He looked around for an escape route, but there was none. He was caught dead to right. If he tried to run, he would become Swiss cheese for sure, riddled with bullet holes. He put his hands in the air to surrender.

Allen got out of the car calmly. He reached into his pocket and pulled out his badge. JR was dumbfounded and amazed. All of this time, he had a federal agent right up under his nose, and he had no clue. He thought Allen was a naïve college student, and come to find out, he was an agent that played his part to the letter.

"Nigel Hawkins Jr., you're under arrest. You have the right to remain silent. Anything you say can and will be used against you," Allen stated as he read him his Miranda rights.

"You're an agent? Get the fuck outta here! This can't be real," JR swore.

"It is real, JR. I'm sorry to disappoint you, my friend," Allen stated resolutely. He placed JR in handcuffs.

"Your ass is dead, you hear me? I'm putting a contract on your head! I don't care what it cost. Your ass is done!" JR promised him. He spit on Allen to display his disgust. He took Allen under his wing and looked out for him like he was his little brother, only to find out that the whole story about him being a struggling college student was just a cover. JR was more embarrassed about being duped by the Feds than he was about being arrested for murder and drug charges. It was a fatal blow to his ego.

"Threatening a federal agent? Well, that's just one more charge we can add on top of all the others you're facing," Allen shot back, unfazed by JR's threatening tactics. He had been threatened before by suspects, so this was nothing new.

"Well, well if it isn't the notorious JR Hawkins. The big man and head honcho in handcuffs. Mr. Money Kings himself right here in the flesh. It looks like your luck has run out," Anderson stated with a wide-eyed grin.

"Fuck you, pig. My lawyers are gonna hand you my ass to kiss once they get done tearing your case apart. This is entrapment," JR stated defiantly

"Not this time, my friend. You see, thanks to your

father, we have all of the information that we need to lock you away for a long, long time. All of these years we've been trying to catch you talking shop on the phone and all it took was for daddy dearest to chat you up and we got you hook line and sinker," Anderson boasted.

"Oh, and my partner forgot to mention how your wife's testimony is gonna be the nail in the coffin for you," Parks chimed in.

JR couldn't believe what he just heard. There was no way in hell that Rochelle would sell him out. She was his ride or die chick. If nobody else held him down, she sure would. This had to be another mind game they were running on him.

"Yeah, okay, pigs. My wife would never cross me. You're just grabbing at straws," JR argued.

"There was a time that might have been true. But once she saw those pics of you getting some of Roshonda's jungle booty in all of those freaky positions, she ran to us to give us everything she knew about your organization. And we threatened to take away your kids, that was all the convincing she needed to cooperate," Parks added.

After hearing those words, JR knew that what they said was true. Rochelle had turned her back on him. Being honest, he had put her in a position where she had no choice.

He was placed in a squad car in handcuffs and carted away. JR's reign on the throne was officially over. He was king no more.

26

JR's arrest made national news. Agents Anderson and Parks reveled in the spotlight as they were touted as heroes in the media for being successful in breaking up one of the largest national drug rings in US history. The only down side of their case was that they were unable to get an indictment against Julio. Even with all of Senator Connors' pull in the political arena behind their investigation, they ran into a stalemate when it came time to bringing charges against Julio. It turns out that this Colombian drug lord had more pull than a United States senator did, in his own damn country. They were told by Senator Connors off the record that someone high up in the Colombian government had influential friends close to the President of the United States, who intervened on his behalf. He was given diplomatic immunity from prosecution. Despite this major setback, all was not lost for them. They both were promoted to a higher pay grade, in exchange for not pursuing further charges against Julio. They both gladly accepted the worthy consolation prize.

After several rounds of legal wrangling, JR's attorney, Martin Rhodes finally got him to agree to take a plea deal instead of facing trial. If he went to trial, he would face the death penalty. Given the mountain high pile of direct evidence that the Feds had that linked him to international drug trafficking, multiple murders, running a continuing criminal enterprise, and income tax evasion, he would be convicted on every count swiftly if this case went before a jury. The public wanted nothing more than to see a drug dealing social pariah like JR face death for all of the lives that the drugs he disbursed across the country destroyed. JR paid Martin Rhodes a hefty amount of money in legal fees, but that still wasn't enough money to beat this case.

The best that Martin could negotiate for him was life in prison with the death penalty taken off the table. In exchange for this compromise, all JR had to give them was information on the location of all of his plants that manufactured Molly pills up and down the East Coast. JR gave up the information they requested, but he refused to implicate Julio in any way, shape, or form. He took full responsibility for setting up the pill operation himself. He refused to admit that Julio had any involvement at all. At this point, he had nothing to lose by taking the full weight for the charge. He remained firm in this position, no matter how many coercion tactics they used on him. Julio had played the game fair with him in all of their business dealings and he couldn't live with taking him down with him. They did business with honor, as gangsters were supposed to do, and he refused to violate the code of the streets that he swore his allegiance to for life. Even in defeat, JR was determined to go out like a true G.

The one thing that hurt JR the most about his legal situation was the fact that he would never see his sons or little brother again. After Nicole and Nigel's deaths, Franklin stepped up to the plate to get custody of Malachi. As his uncle, he wanted to ensure that he had a strong male role model in his life to emulate, so that he wouldn't go down the same negative path as his father and brother.

JR would get over Rochelle's giving him up to the Feds in time, because he had put her through hell through the years. He didn't blame her for her choice to take care of his boys over being loyal to him. Any good mother would do the same thing for her children. He loved all three of them with all of his heart, no matter what evil deeds he did out in the streets. The only solace he could find in not being able to see their handsome faces anymore was that they would be safe from harm in Rochelle's care. He never doubted her abilities as a good mother. The only memory that he would have of his boys would be the few pictures he had in his cell. He looked at them daily as a reminder of the two good things that he did do in his life. For a man facing twenty-three hours of every day inside of a cell for the rest of his life, a positive thought was worth more than any material possession.

"Hawkins, it's time to go," the CO yelled into JR's cell.

JR got up from his bunk to exit his cell. He was dressed in a dark blue Italian suit and looked like a businessman, instead of a street thug on his way to court. Today was the day that he was scheduled to appear before the court and enter his official plea of guilty to all charges, and to accept the terms of his plea-bargain agreement. This would be the last time he would wear civilian clothes in his life, so he made sure that Martin got him the most expensive tailor made suit he could find. It would be his last reminder of the good life he used to live. He used to be able to afford the most expensive and finest clothing that was made all over the world, but from here on out, the clothes he wore wouldn't come from the world's most famous fashion houses. Instead, it would be government issued prison gear.

"Man, I'ma enjoy this fresh air. Can you take the long way to the court house so that I can enjoy it for as long as possible?" JR asked the CO.

"Hawkins, get ya ass over here so I can put these cuffs on you so I can get you over to the court house," the CO replied. He ignored his request. As far as he was concerned, JR was just another criminal piece of shit that deserved no special treatment.

JR did as instructed. The officer cuffed his hands behind him and escorted him down the corridor. He stopped to chat briefly with another CO on the way to the transportation van. When they reached the van, JR was assisted in the back of the van. They exited the jail en route to the courthouse. JR enjoyed the ride through the streets of Baltimore. He reminisced about all of the hell he had raised out in them, and all the fun he had, spending tons of money on the finest women, cars, and clothes. He had lived a lifestyle that very few men get a chance to live. He had no regrets about his choices in life. He believed that his path in life was ordained for him from the time he was born.

When they reached the courthouse, various media outlets were all over the front area. They were eager to get any kind of statement or photograph of JR that they could. When he stepped out of the van, the flash of cameras everywhere and microphones being shoved in his face made him chuckle inside. The correctional officers attempted to act as a barrier between him and the press. They were pushed and shoved by the sizable crowd. It wasn't just the press that was out there, JR had many young hustlers that looked up to him still, and they wanted one last glimpse at their hero.

In spite of the pending doom of his current situation, JR took pride in receiving so much attention. He loved the notoriety. It gave him a rush inside like drugs could never do. He had overdosed on power long ago, and it ultimately led to his demise and downfall.

When he reached the main entrance of the courthouse, a man wearing a press badge had managed to break through the crowd and get between him and the correctional officers. He caught JR off guard, because he was able to get close enough to him to whisper in his ear.

"This is from Julio, my friend," the man said in a tone low enough for only JR to hear over the loud noise made by the crowd.

Right after he said those words, the man shoved his knife into JR's chest. His blade went straight into JR's heart. One of the COs grabbed the man instantly and pinned him to the ground. The crowd screamed in hysteria when they witnessed JR fall to the ground with his hands over his chest, covered in blood. This would be his last chance enjoy the spotlight. He looked out into the crowd and smiled as he took his last breath. He died on the courthouse steps, a victim of the same brutal violence that he had perpetuated virtually his entire adult life.

Even though he didn't snitch on Julio, he still saw him as a potential threat to change his mind later on and decide to make a deal with the Feds after the wear and tear, and the isolation of prison life took its toll on him. Julio wasn't willing to take the chance that he would remain steadfast as a soldier, so he decided that he needed to be dealt with now. This was the life that JR chose to live, and it was this same lifestyle that ended his life. He stayed loyal to the game, but the game wasn't loyal to him in the end. All the money and the power couldn't save him from the hands of karma when she dealt out her sweet justice.

Thomas Long

Coming spring 2014!

MR. UNTOUCHABLE
A THUG'S LIFE PT. 2

www.ingramcontent.com/pod-product-compliance
Lightning Source LLC
Chambersburg PA
CBHW050040180626
46810CB00002B/815